MONSTER'S PRICE

Pizza Shop Monster Hunter
Book 1

By
Dakota Brown

Monster's Price
A Why Choose Tale

Pizza Shop Monster Hunter, Book 1

Inkwolf Press
P.O. Box 473
Ault, Colorado
80610

ISBN: 979-8-9864144-5-4

www.inkwolfpress.com

PRODUCED IN THE UNITED STATES OF AMERICA

10 9 8 7 6 5 4 3 2 1

DEDICATION

This one's for all the Pizza Shop fans!
I wrote this for you.

Author's Note

This is an existing group of men. If you want to read how
they all met, you'll have to check out the Pizza Shop
Exorcist Series. However, this book is a stand-alone
adventure in that world, and can be read and enjoyed
without having read the other series.

ACKNOWLEDGEMENTS

First off, thank you all for asking me for this book. I might not have written it without the continued encouragement and requests from everyone who loves this series. I'm really happy with how it came out, and I hope you enjoy it as well.

Nextly, thank you everyone who helped put this book together. In no particular order. My proofers: Michelle, Andrea, Kristen. My Alpha Team: Angie, Chelsi, Janet, Kelly, Michael, Sarah, Stacy. And my editor: Lynn.

A special thanks goes out to Aeryn Havens. Can I even write a novel without you? I don't know anymore. Love you.

Thanks always go to my awesome PA: Becky Hodges. I appreciate everything you do.

I also want to thank Shoshanah for all her wonderful brainstorming that went into the backstory.

And last but never least, thank you to my patrons on Patreon: Tina, Museholly, Nina, Latisha, Kelly, Ruby, Julie, Arkay, Tabitha, Wendy, Allison, Michael, Rachael, Teri, Shay, Jacqui, Melynda, Yashira

CHAPTER 1

Price

"**I**s this really necessary?" I tugged at my leather jacket and shifted, butterflies fluttering uncomfortably in my stomach.

"Yes, Chris Price, it's necessary." Lucifer's smoothly seductive voice normally would have filled me with a different sort of butterfly, but right now, all I could hear was amusement covering the seduction, and I wanted to punch him.

"It is not. You just want to torture me," I grumbled.

"Maybe," the ruler of Hell allowed. "We need to find out more about what exactly we let loose when we destroyed the wards at the Vatican, and this is a perfect opportunity." He sounded far too cheerful about the situation.

"You're taking me to tea. With the pope! I assure you he doesn't want to see me." I glared at my mate.

"He wants to see me even less." The devil winked. "It'll be fun."

"Fuck," I muttered, knowing I wasn't going to win this one. I could outright refuse, but he was at least sort of right.

He chuckled. "Say goodbye to the others, and we'll get out of here."

1

I flipped him off and glanced around my basement that was half occult workshop, with the permanent silver circle inlaid into my specially sealed floor to keep out any cracks or imperfections, and half a living space for Brennan, my half-fae mate who was the real mage of the group. My Pomeranian-shaped hellhound sat at my feet and woofed softly.

"The others are all asleep, mate. Well, except for Aaron, who's insane." Aaron was my Nephilim mate, and the only one of us who was a morning person. He worked at the government lab nearby and also had a ton of excess energy from his nature, so he usually ran or worked out in the morning on his way to work.

Ezra, my demon prince mate, was in Hell in his domain, asleep by the feeling through the marks I shared with him, and I knew Mal and Sabian were out cold. Mal was a vampire and though he wasn't constrained to the night like popular legend might lead one to believe, he was certainly nocturnal by nature. Sabian was whatever he needed to be, but since the incubus had modeled at least some of his behavior off my preferences, he was also not a morning person. They were both passed out in the main bedroom where I'd recently been until my alarm woke me. It had woken them too, but they'd been unconscious again by the time I'd left. Bastards.

Instead of answering, Lucifer held out his hand.

Continuing to glare, I put mine in his. His skin heated my cool hand, and he pulled me into his arms. The devil cupped the back of my head with one hand and dug the fingers of his other hand into my ass cheek, squeezing not entirely gently.

I pressed against him, groaning softly as he leaned in for a kiss.

Maybe if I distract him enough... I slid one leg up against his and dug my fingers into his back.

He rumbled appreciatively, but my tactic, enjoyable as it was, didn't work. After a gentle nip at my lower lip, he released me with a mischievous glint in his eyes. "Maybe later." He kept hold of one of my hands as if to keep me from bolting.

I snorted in reply. "Not going to be in the mood later, mate. Not after what is likely to be the most uncomfortable encounter of my life."

Lucifer laughed. "Let's go." He held out his free hand and gestured. A stream of dark red energy spiraled into a disk, then expanded into a portal that presumably would let us out in Rome, Italy.

"I have not had enough caffeine for this," I grumbled as I followed Lucifer through the portal, Mayhem on my heels. Technically, only Lucifer could create portals anywhere he liked in the mortal realm. All lesser demons either had to go through a portal he created, or one of the handful of permanent ones scattered throughout the world. Angels had different rules, and I didn't fully understand them, but I knew archangels could travel as freely as Lucifer did. I say technically, because I could also create portals at a whim, though I wasn't nearly as practiced at it as Lucifer. Ezra, who was *only* a demonic prince, was also gaining the ability to portal freely due to our bonds. This was not something we were spreading around.

We stepped out the other side of the portal and the warm, humid air of Rome slapped me in the face, contrasting sharply with the cool, dry air in my basement.

Unlike when we'd come here before and exited our portal in an alley near the walls around Vatican City, Lucifer had brought us right into the courtyard in front of the Papal Palace.

Much to numerous people's dismay.

The devil chuckled in amusement.

I sighed.

3

The last time I'd been here, I really hadn't taken much time to look around. Now I spent a moment turning in a slow circle, taking in the ancient architecture and how it melded, or in some cases didn't, with the needs of a modern society. Tourists milled about, some obviously lost, some overcome with emotions. Others were clearly on tours, while members of the clergy hurried about on whatever business they had.

We'd come out in a grassy courtyard. I was a little amazed that we didn't have everyone's attention. Most of the tourists were focused on something that looked like a giant pinecone in a planter. Or was that a giant brass ball? I had to be missing something, but I quickly suppressed the joke that wanted to leap out of my mouth lest I find out if the priests gaping at us understood English. Commenting on the pope's single brass ball was probably not the way to win friends here.

One of the priests—I really didn't know their ranks at all—pointed at me and shouted angrily. I thought I recognized him from my last visit and applied a touch of power so I could understand Italian. He was condemning me as a demon. Okay, maybe I did understand a hint of Lucifer's amusement. I tried to suppress the smile that threatened to curl my lips and only partially succeeded. Maybe I should have made the joke.

"I am here for tea." Lucifer's cultured voice sounded extra sexy in Italian.

"Tea?" the priest sputtered. Or, well, I really didn't know his rank or title, so I was sticking with priest.

"Yes, with the pope, of course."

"Of course," the priest sneered. He was a younger man, hair still full and dark, with a strong nose and piercing eyes. He wore robes like most of the other clergy as I'd come to expect from Catholics, though his had some sort of design embroidered on the black collar of his shirt that didn't mean anything to me. I'd never seen it before, ever, on a priest. I blinked, and the design was gone. Weird. *Magic?*

"Are you expected? I don't believe the pope has time in his schedule for random visitors." The haughty expression on the priest's face was calculating and not nearly as shocked as I would have expected after a couple of people appeared out of nowhere.

Of course, I'd been here recently, and so had a bunch of other demons, a vampire, and a couple of archangels, so maybe they weren't actually shocked.

"I assure you, he is not expecting myself, or Ms. Price, but I also assure you he will see us."

"And you are?" the priest who'd just called me a demon asked stiffly.

"Mr. Morningstar."

The priest's eyes narrowed. He crossed himself and said a fervent prayer, but I'd expected a great deal more fear. It wasn't every day the devil showed up on your doorstep. Well, unless you were me. I almost didn't stop the laugh that tried to escape my lips.

"Do hurry along. I don't have all day." Lucifer made a shooing motion with his hand.

I could see the debate in the poor priest's eyes. Did he try to cast us out? Or let someone else deal with us?

Finally, he tightened his lips, gaze flicking down to Mayhem before he sighed. "Come with me."

He led us down a path through the well-tended green, around a handful of security checkpoints and into the main entry into the palace. Even here tourists milled about. We avoided them and took a few side hallways before the priest gave us another dark look and left us in a receiving room.

My gaze flicked over the relics and pictures and other riches that cluttered the walls in the comfortable room.

Lucifer sank down into a chair, crossed his legs, and sat waiting with the utmost patience.

I wandered over to the bookshelf and studied the titles, expecting to be kept waiting. When the door opened shortly after, I turned, startled by the quick response.

"I'm surprised you can enter this place, Adversary." An older, distinguished-looking man dressed in official-looking flowing white robes entered alone. His hair still had hints of a darker shade through the steel that colored it, and though clearly well fed, there was a suggestion of what might have once been an athletic build lingering in his visage.

"Hello, Holy Father. Of course, I can enter here. I am, after all, still an angel." Lucifer rose from his chair and bowed ever so slightly.

"I see. And you are here for tea?" The man managed to keep his emotions behind a mask, though I read a hint of uneasiness in the set of his shoulders.

"Yes. And a discussion."

"I assumed. Tea will be along shortly. And your companion?"

"Pope John, this is my friend, Chris Price. Exorcist."

The pope's eyes narrowed, and the stare he turned on me might have turned my blood into ice if I hadn't faced down demons on their own turf and survived. Might still have, if I hadn't had the most powerful demon in existence standing at my side.

"Nice to meet you, mate," I said with a cocky grin. Fighting discomfort with sarcasm and wit, one awkward situation at a time, that was me.

"The pleasure is all yours, I assure you," the pope replied before gesturing toward a table. "Please, take a seat. Ms. Price, I believe you've been here before."

I shrugged. "Yeah, unfortunately."

That comment elicited a tight smile. "Agreed."

We sat at a round table with a plain white cloth covering the wooden top. Mayhem lay down at my feet, alert for trouble. I seemed to recall affording him some sort of shielding the last time we were here that kept him safe from all the holy energy, and he acted quite comfortable.

A soft knock on the door stopped the conversation.

"Come in," the pope called.

A younger man came in, pushing a silver tea cart. I wasn't sure if he was a household servant or another priest, or how things worked in the Vatican. Did you have to be ordained to serve tea to the pope?

Pushing that irrelevant question away, I watched as the guy expertly set out the tea service, every motion precise. He followed with a plate of finger-sized sandwiches and some sort of dessert biscuit.

"Will it offend you if I say a quick word over our meal?" The pope's inscrutable smile didn't reach his eyes. For a moment, I thought Pope John's collar shimmered with the same sigil I'd noticed on the other priest's outfit. Then it was gone. Totally weird.

"Not at all, Your Holiness." Lucifer's smile was equally enigmatic.

I could feel a trickle of power that tapped into a much deeper well flow through the pope's blessing and suspected that while Lucifer said it wouldn't be a problem for him, a less angelic demon wouldn't fare well at all. Good to know. I avoided glancing at Mayhem. I didn't want anyone who hadn't already guessed his nature to clue into it. He felt fine through our bond, however.

We all poured our own tea, and after a quick glance at my demonic companion, I took a sip. It was a nice black tea, and the sandwiches were excellent.

"My predecessor warned me that I should expect a visit from you at some point or another. I nearly didn't believe him, until the events of a few months ago,

7

anyway." Pope John kept his tone conversational, but I could hear an undercurrent of anger.

"They were trying to start the apocalypse, mate. We stopped it." I did my best not to let anger into my voice, as he had, but it was there all the same.

"Though people always hope for signs from above, our faith should be more than sufficient to convince us of the truth of our religion. Even with the previous pope's warning, I had not expected to meet two archangels, the devil, a handful of demons, an exorcist, and a hellhound in short order." His gaze strayed toward Mayhem for a moment.

"To be fair, same." I hesitated. "Well, except for the demons. I'd met a few of them in the past. Exorcist and all."

That didn't impress Pope John, and he fixed his gaze on me for a moment. "Why did you choose to bring her along on your visit?"

"It was not entirely Chris's fault, what happened with the wards on the Vatican. She has agreed to help recover the beings that escaped. I thought it would be best if she were here when you told us what exactly now roamed the mortal realms."

"And why would I tell you?" Pope John took a sip of his tea.

"So we know what we're up against," Lucifer replied, brow furrowed in confusion.

"Ahh, but you see, Adversary, we put them in their metaphysical prison once before. We will do so again. The Vatican does not require, or even prefer, your assistance."

"Well, I'd be just as happy to leave it to you, but I'm afraid Gabriel insisted. While I'm not normally a fan of listening to archangels, they did us a good turn and I agreed." Lucifer leaned back in his chair, teacup forgotten on the table.

The pope grimaced, though I wasn't sure if it was because Lucifer mentioned Gabriel, or because he was using the gender-neutral phrasing. The Catholics had a pretty narrow view of the gender of their holy beings, and yet the beings themselves were a great deal more fluid. At least in my somewhat limited experience.

"He suggested the same to me."

I straightened, and Lucifer shot me a look. I stifled my anger and let the slight slide.

"But we are not interested in any sort of alliance with the devil, even one born of the recent circumstances. That road leads to damnation. Something you should consider well." He turned that last comment on me.

"Eh." I shrugged. "Last I heard, my soul was still safe. It was an archangel who told me, so I guess I'm pretty comfortable with my choices."

That got a pair of raised eyebrows from the pope.

"Things are not so black and white as you might hope," Lucifer said.

"All the same, leave the recovery to us. Is that all?" He stood and gestured toward the door.

"There are many other topics we might discuss. I will pay you another visit in the future. One in which you will ask for my assistance. I know of some of the creatures you harbored because I put them behind your wards in the first place. Look back in your records a few centuries. Rest assured; I will find a more suitable prison for them this time." Lucifer steepled his fingers, considering the pope, and unconcerned about the dismissal.

"Chris Price, I will pray for your soul. Though you may consider yourself unwelcome in our churches." Pope John's tone was gracious, though it carried a hint of his anger at the end.

"Nothing new there." I stood, wondering if that meant I was officially getting excommunicated. Not being

9

Catholic, I had no idea what the rules were for that. Not that I cared.

Lucifer also got to his feet, though more slowly than I did.

"Consider your history, John," Lucifer commanded, before striding toward the door. I fell in next to him, though he did hold the door for me.

"Seriously not enough caffeine for that," I muttered once we were out in the grand entryway.

"I will take you someplace to make up for it," he answered just as quietly.

He didn't make a portal inside the Papal Palace, instead waiting until we were outside, apparently not concerned with an audience. We stepped through, and I hoped wherever we came out, the caffeine would be decadent.

CHAPTER 2

Price

"This is the best coffee I've ever had." I savored the aroma almost as much as the taste of the delicious brew cradled in my hands. Mayhem lay at my feet. Lucifer had taken me to a café in Thailand. I never would have expected that to be a place to get the best coffee I'd ever had. Apparently, the country was famous for it.

"Worth the trip to Rome?" Lucifer had his own mug, and he held it carefully in one hand while he watched me enjoying mine.

We sat on a wooden deck that overlooked a canal. The shop behind us was modern, but also held onto the local flavor of the country. A few tourists and a handful of Thai people drank their brews on the deck or in the shop under fans. It was humid, and I'd given in and cast the spell that let me basically ignore the elements. Cheating, yes, but I was a desert girl, and I did not get along with the humidity at all.

I stared into his dark eyes and tried to ignore his infectious smile. It didn't completely work.

"I don't know. I can think of a few other things that might help make me feel better, too."

"Oh, really?" He arched one elegant eyebrow, his eyes glinting with mischief.

I licked my lips and took another drink, keeping eye contact with my mate over the rim of the mug.

His grin widened. "Perhaps a tour of a particularly dank set of catacombs in search of a ghoul or two as practice for going after more difficult monsters?"

Shaking my head, I broke eye contact and leaned back in my chair to down the rest of the coffee. The delicious pastries we'd gotten were nothing but crumbs and a happy memory, and I was ready to get back home. "No catacombs, thank you."

I didn't want to know how the owner of this particular shop had come to Lucifer's attention. He hadn't acted surprised to see the demon. Just me. I'd come to Lucifer's attention because my demon prince, Ezra, introduced us when we needed passage into Hell to rescue my incubus from the demon who had stolen him away from me.

Lucifer frowned, straightening, just as power surged from my center outward through my wards, throwing out a wave of defensive energy. Lucifer threw himself back against the wall of the building we sat outside and shielded himself. Which might have saved him some trouble, as I hadn't noticed the person sneaking up behind him until the demon moved. Said individual was tossed like a rag doll by the blast of defensive magic that my powerful wards let off. He splashed into the water, which was a terrible place for an unconscious person to end up. I leaped out of my chair and spun around, wondering who or what had set them off.

Another man lay on the ground about ten feet behind me, unconscious. He was a white man and wore everyday clothing, jeans, a t-shirt, and hiking boots.

The blast from my wards had taken out a few tables, and one couple had spilled their coffee. Mayhem shifted to his hellhound form and stalked the unconscious man.

Lucifer went on damage control, and I left him to it. Before I investigated the unconscious person on the deck, I went over to the edge and peered into the murky water, but I didn't see the other man at all. Either he was gone for good, or the water had woken him, and he'd swam away. I wasn't going to try to find out.

Demon magic had the rest of the chaos under control when I returned to the now awake man who had triggered my wards. His features were as unremarkable as his clothing, except perhaps that he was white instead of Thai. His sandy hair and blue eyes would have fit in any European country. The anger that narrowed his eyes when he looked at me, and the absolute disgust he leveled at Lucifer, made me think he knew exactly who and what we were. *Interesting.* Mayhem, in all his demonic glory, didn't seem to faze him at all.

Of course, fear would have been more logical than disgust.

"And who might you be?" Lucifer stood over the man, rage flickering in the form of hellfire in the demon's eyes. The depth of his emotion was otherwise masked by a bland expression.

The man didn't reply. Couldn't say I was surprised.

"My dear, can you find your own way home?" Lucifer reached down and grabbed the man's shirt. Our target's eyes finally gave the first hint of fear.

"I suppose," I sighed. Though I knew I could get laid when I got home, I'd hoped for some time with my devil. I didn't get to see him as often as I did the others, and since we hadn't renewed our shared marks, I felt his absence more keenly than my other mates. That was a matter I hoped to address with him, soon. I'd rather impertinently put my own version of a demon mark on the ruler of Hell after he'd taught me how. He'd not been pleased, but I'd done it after he'd already given me his own demon mark.

Unfortunately, our first set of marks had been stripped away by Mammon in his attempt to take over my soul, and Hell. The second set had been destroyed by most of my men getting effectively killed by the same demon. Once I'd saved everyone, I'd renewed my marks with all my other men. There was a rather prominent empty circle on my chest between my breasts where Lucifer's should have been. I wanted it back, and I wanted my pizza pentagram mark back on his forearm. Yes, I realize that was insane, but the last few months had been nuts, so I was just going with it.

Lucifer again made a portal and dragged my attacker through it before he could protest. Again, no one reacted. Was the devil doing some sort of magic to keep people from noticing? If so, I needed to figure out the spell because it was far better than anything I'd managed so far.

Not knowing what else to do, I wandered off the patio and into the crowded streets, my hellhound at my side. He was doing his invisible dog routine, which worked even in demonic form. The shouts of the vendors, the aromas of the local food, and the crush of the people enveloped me, and I enjoyed being somewhere completely different than home for a time.

There were fewer cars here than in a major city, and the air was fresh. I let my thoughts meander as I enjoyed the lush scenery mixed with the hustle and bustle of humanity. Unsurprisingly, I caught more than a few curious looks. Black combat boots and ripped, acid-washed jeans were already out of place, but the leather jacket with the anarchy symbol on the front and the Price's Pizza Parlor pizza pentacle logo on the back was enough to get notice in the US, let alone outside it. Not to mention we were in a hot, tropical environment, and I wasn't sweating. Topping off the look was my hair, long on top, shaved sides, and bleached blond, and all the tattoos that were visible anywhere I showed skin below my neck. Yeah, no one had ever accused me of being subtle.

I wandered for a while longer, taken with the charm of the city I strolled through. Unfortunately, the laundry list of things I needed to do before our grand re-opening at the pizza parlor intruded on my thoughts.

A few months back when we'd been fighting archangels and saving the world, my pizza shop had been burned to the ground. While I'd been tempted to magic it back into existence, enough people had seen it destroyed by the time I'd had a second to think about it, that we'd decided just to let it be rebuilt the normal way. I might have used magic to speed things along, however. Or maybe my demonic connections, or a little of both. I wasn't about to admit to any of that. Not at all.

We had just passed all our mundane world inspections and Ezra, Mal, and Brennan had laid down some serious wards that should keep us plenty protected from anything supernatural, including archangels.

Now I just needed to finalize some details and get my staff up to speed. I hoped they'd enjoyed their extended vacation. I'd paid everyone who wanted to come back while we'd been shut down. A few of my employees had gone on to other things, but most of them were coming back. One of the secrets to the success at Price's Pizza Parlor was a very satisfied staff.

Cursing the devil, I found a secluded spot between a couple of buildings and pulled on my powers to form a portal.

It didn't completely surprise me when I failed.

"Fuck," I growled.

This type of magic was not my strong suit. I could do it, but it went wrong about as often as it went right. About the only time I was really reliable was when I was under duress, and then I tended to grab so much power that there was no way it could fail. I had very little subtlety, especially with magic. Me, yeah, I was a sledgehammer.

The only place that didn't apply was exorcisms. I could be a sledgehammer, but I had years of practice at careful extractions, too.

A couple more tries and a couple more failures had me gritting my teeth and clenching my hands, so I sent out a call for Inferno, my nightstallion. If nothing else, he could fly me home reasonably quickly.

I sensed him respond to my call, so I left the alley and continued wandering down the street. He'd meet me as soon as he could. Until then, I would enjoy taking in the sights of some place I'd never been before, my hellhound at my side.

***

About an hour later, as I took in the open markets and all the wares for sale, Mayhem stopped suddenly, spinning around, a low growl in his throat.

Tightening my lips in annoyance and gathering power to me, I turned. A tall, lean woman stalked toward me, the press of humanity parting around her as if she used magic on them to clear a path. She had short blond hair, stormy gray eyes, and grace to her movement. I suspected she was either a dancer of some sort or a martial artist. She wore a white suit with a black tie and was as out of place in this environment as I was.

Her brow was furrowed in a deep frown and something about the way she carried herself made me think that was her normal expression, and not just for me in particular.

Though I doubted I'd ever be the one to get a smile from her.

"You are rather hard on people around you," she snapped as she approached. "Where is Brady?"

"Who the hell is Brady, mate? And who the hell are you?" I put my fists on my hips and glared back.

"Yashira." She pointed a finger at her chest. "Brady was sent to have a discussion with you, along with Stanton. Who returned. Wet. So, where's Brady?"

"Uh, probably not having a very good time in Hell. Why?"

She rocked back in surprise. "You killed him?"

"No, but when you attack the devil, then refuse to answer his questions, he can pretty much do whatever he wants with you." I had no idea what the rules actually were, or if Lucifer had taken Brady to Hell or not, but she didn't need to know that.

Yashira went quiet for a moment before continuing. "You think the devil will trade your life for Brady's?"

I snorted, my gaze drifting to a fishing boat loaded down with the day's catch cruising by on the river. "I think if you tried that, you'd end up dead and so would Brady."

She studied me for a moment. "Perhaps. What will it take to get him returned?"

"Information. Who the fuck are you people and why are you randomly attacking us in Thailand, of all places?" I snapped at her. Mayhem growled. "Hell, how did you track us down? We only just got here."

"We are everywhere," she replied with the faintest of smiles.

"And who the fuck are you?"

"The righteous."

Her gaze slid toward the hellhound and her frown deepened. Then she turned and strode away, the press of locals closing in around her.

"Well, that was fucking weird as fuck." I rubbed my hand over my face as I watched her leave. "I guess she didn't want to rescue Brady after all."

Mayhem gave another low rumble before looking up.

"Finally," I breathed out as I saw my fiery stallion sailing out of the sky toward me. Inferno was a nightstallion, a demonic version of the spirit horses that the Riders of the Apocalypse rode. He had chosen me to be his rider and generally stuck around, though occasionally he went off to Hell for a few days. I'd never thought I'd like having a horse around, but I really enjoyed Inferno. Not that he was a horse, but I did ride him either in his equine form or his motorcycle form. The spirit horses all took the shape of sport bikes. Inferno was apparently a Harley fan, though, because he mimicked a road bike.

The big black creature landed next to me, and I rubbed his forehead when he lowered his head, hoping he was camouflaging himself with magic or we were about to get a lot of attention.

"Hi, buddy," I said.

He nickered.

"You two ready to get home?" By the lack of screaming, Inferno was cloaking us.

Mayhem woofed softly.

I ran my hand down Inferno's smooth, muscled neck and tangled my fingers in his flaming mane. Though I knew the flames that licked his mane, tail, and his legs could burn, they'd never hurt me.

His magic gripped me and lifted me rapidly onto his back. It was almost like being teleported onto the nightstallion. The spirit horses had a similar power, but they all made their riders learn to mount properly. Inferno took pity on me. He was damn tall, and I was not a natural equestrian.

I leaned forward and petted his neck before wrapping my hands in his mane. Inferno leaped into the air, Mayhem following, the hellhound also able to fly with us, and headed for home.

The trip wouldn't take as long as it would on an airplane, but it would be a little while before we were back in Santa Fe, so I settled in for the ride. Enjoying the quiet and peace of being in the air with two of my closest companions. Inferno's inherent magic protected me from the elements, otherwise I'd freeze without my own magic. He deadened the wind and made the trip incredibly peaceful.

If you'd have told me a year ago that I'd be doing any of the things I did now, I'd have laughed in your face. I was an exorcist. I didn't fuck demons, I banished them. Well, now I did both, and a lot of other things besides.

We'd stopped an apocalypse, battled demons and archangels, and I supposed that was more than enough for any lifetime. If the Vatican didn't want my help, well, that was on them.

Lucifer had promised Gabriel we would help put the creatures I'd let loose away, but I wasn't exactly in a hurry to make good on that, especially since I wasn't actually responsible for cleaning up that mess. No, I had a pizza shop to run and a bunch of yummy men to, uh, hang out with.

Even if one of them had left me in Thailand without a portal home.

Dakota Brown

CHAPTER 3

Price

Garlic, tomato, yeasty dough, and the heat of the pizza ovens, these were the smells of my childhood, and it was so good to have everything back online. We were having a pizza party and training for all the employees. Billy, my manager, had a gigantic grin on his face as he went from employee to employee, making sure they had everything they needed, from uniforms to information. The cooks were practicing our signature recipes and everyone else was taking turns roleplaying taking orders, being customers, and generally having a good time.

I had the music turned up, though not so loud that we couldn't talk. Sabian had decided he wanted to learn how to run the place as another assistant manager and he shadowed Billy. Brennan, Aaron, and Mal sat at a booth near the door with Mayhem curled up in his fluffy yellow form on the seat next to the vampire. Brennan and Aaron were taste-testing the pizza while Mal sipped on a beer. He and Brennan were testing the wards.

We had invited a few select customers to stop by for the training run in about an hour, and I looked forward to seeing what they thought of the rebuilt shop.

Though I'd kept much of the décor the same, eighties memorabilia—some recreated through magic, some tracked down from various online vendors—I'd added a wood stove for wood-fired pizza, and a small eighties-style arcade that still ran on quarters, and a bar that overlooked the kitchen for people who didn't want to sit at a table.

21

We'd added a little more space when we had rebuilt.

I was loving it. My experienced cooks were learning how to use the wood oven, and I went over to join them. "How's it going?"

Cassandra grinned at me while tossing dough in the air. "Good to be back, boss."

"Glad to hear it."

The secret to Price's Pizza Parlor's continued success was fabulous pizza and happy staff.

I caught sight of Mandy heading over to check on my guys. She still blushed when she looked at Mal, but now that she had her own incubus to keep her happy, she wasn't as wide-eyed when she was around my vampire. He'd rescued her from a kidnapping attempt a few months ago, and she'd learned far more about our world than I'd have preferred. Of course, most of the staff knew what my men were, and had all promised to keep their mouths shut. The new folks didn't know, and hopefully they wouldn't have to find out.

The bells on the door chimed and, since I was still watching Mandy, I saw her freeze. Slowly, dreading what I might find, I turned so I could see what had attracted her attention. A child walked through the door. Or rather, an angelic being wearing a child's body. It was impossible to determine the being's gender from hairstyle, clothing, or even the soft ageless features. The child-like archangel got a fair bit of attention from my staff, some because they knew who Gabriel was, and some because a child had apparently walked into the shop alone.

"Fuck," I muttered and hurried into the dining area.

Mandy went over to the angel and took them to the booth my guys were at. The guys made room, and by the time I got there, Mandy was taking their order.

"Gabriel," I said in greeting.

"Hello, Chris Price." Gabriel sat serenely; hands folded on the tabletop.

"What brings you to our establishment?" I glanced at Mal. I'd thought he'd warded against angels.

Mal caught my gaze but didn't act perturbed. Maybe he'd made an exception for Gabriel? I'd find out later.

"I thought I'd try your new wood-fired pizza," the angel replied with a deadpan expression I couldn't interpret.

"Ahh. Should we expect anyone else esoteric?" That was the nicest way I could think of to say it.

This brought a smile to their face. "No."

I couldn't quite stifle my sigh of relief. "Don't get me wrong, I'm glad to see you. Just…" I waved my hand at the shop. "We just got it up and running again."

I wasn't sure I'd ever heard the archangel laugh before, but they did now and it made them seem like the youth they portrayed. "I'll bestow our blessings upon this place as well."

I paused for a moment, caught off guard. "Thank you."

They nodded.

Mandy came back with a drink for Gabriel.

"Thank you," they said. "It is good to see you well, Mandy."

Her eyes widened again. "Thank you, Gabriel. I'm glad you were able to stop by and see the new shop."

The door chimed again, and this time it was the first of our expected customers.

"Excuse me for a moment." I went over to act as a hostess to seat them and make sure they knew what their role was for the evening, besides eating tasty free pizza. We were looking for honest feedback and anything we could improve upon. Most of the staff were well seasoned, but if we were going to make any changes, now was the time.

It took almost an hour before I made it back to Gabriel. They seemed content to sit with my men.

"So, how's the pizza, mate?" I squished onto the edge of the booth and Mal put his arm around me, sliding over into Aaron so I could fit temporarily.

"Quite delicious, Chris Price." The angel wiped their hands on a napkin. "I did want to make sure you understood Lucifer's obligation to return the beings he helped you set loose to containment is not your obligation. You are welcome to assist him, but it's not your responsibility."

"That's good to know. Thanks."

They nodded. "I must be off, Chris Price. Thank you for the delicious pizza. I will inform the others that it is quite acceptable." They slid out of the booth.

"My thanks," I said as they left, the door quietly shutting behind them. "Fuck. Does that mean we'll be getting more of their kind of visitors?"

Mal chuckled. "With Ezra's help, Brennan and I managed to adjust the wards so that they would allow friendly supernaturals but repel anyone who had ill intent in their heart. It also nullifies some of their powers within."

"Ohhh, so you turned us into a neutral zone?"

"Essentially."

I sank down into the booth and put my head in my hands. "Mal, I'm not sure if that was brilliant or awful."

Aaron rubbed my back. "Could be interesting."

"I've had enough 'interesting' to last my entire life." I sighed, then got back to my feet. "Well, it's done. Okay. I'll warn Billy."

I wanted to curse at Mal, but he had probably done the right thing. Did I like it? No.

"Hey, boss." Billy glanced up from the register he was showing Sabian how to use, when I came over.

Sabian perked up. "Hi, boss." His tone was nowhere close to professional.

My cheeks heated, and the look in his liquid amber eyes sent that heat straight down into my loins. I cleared my throat. "Sabian, seriously?"

I couldn't even be mad at his happy grin. "Sorry, boss."

His tone this time was only marginally less full of innuendo.

"He's an incubus," Billy pointed out. "I'm not sure he can help it."

I leaned against the counter. "No, probably not. But seriously, do not make me have to get all HR on your sexy ass."

Sabian's grin was far from innocent. I shook my head and returned to the topic on my mind.

"So, uh, some news. Gabriel stopped by, and apparently, they're impressed and about to tell the others that this place is"—I held up my fingers in air quotes— "quite acceptable. We might end up with more visitors of that type. But the wards should still protect the shop and everyone inside."

"Well, no one ever said it was boring around here," Billy replied with a shrug and slid the drawer back into the register. "Keep us on our toes and all." The employees had experienced so much a few months ago, I wasn't completely surprised this didn't faze Billy. From a demon I'd had to exorcise in front of them before they even knew I was an exorcist, to angels trying to abduct Aaron and Mal using blood magic and vampiric powers to fight them off, to a pissed off archangel destroying the place, they'd nearly seen it all.

"Just let everyone know and figure out a way to clue in the newbies without scaring them off."

Billy laughed. "Copy that, boss."

I shook my head and left him and Sabian to their work. Checking in with all my employees, old and new, reassured me. The old hands were taking care of the newbies, and we were really making progress with the pizza party. Some of the trivia night regulars had started up a game, and a few others had discovered the arcade.

I was about to go talk to our guests when the door chimed again.

"Oh boy," I muttered when I saw who it was. Arguably, I'd rather have the archangels than Aaron's parents. We'd invited them out of courtesy. I hadn't actually expected them to come. Aaron was my only partner who had anything like a normal family. I'd met him when we'd rescued him from an evil mage who had tried to use him as a sacrifice in a demonic summoning. Since his house had been burned in the process, and we knew there was something special about him, we'd invited him to stay at my house where he'd be marginally safer.

His parents had been seriously dubious of me before they'd gotten almost zombified by the bad guys and then saved by Ezra who'd claimed their souls before their souls could be stolen away. Once we'd recovered them, with the Angel of Death's help, we'd hidden them away in a place that Azrael called "out of time." To say that we'd had a rocky start was the understatement of the century. Not to mention that I had multiple partners, and they really weren't sure how they felt about that.

Of course, they'd driven up from Albuquerque to visit, so that was awfully nice of them.

"Hi, Patricia. Hello, Martin. How are you two today?" I did my best impression of a customer service voice.

"Hello, Chris," his dad replied, hands stuffed in his pockets and a wary smile on his face. His mom was busy studying the new décor.

"We heard you had wood-fired pizza," she finally said, her gaze finally finding mine. "It's our favorite."

"Why don't you sit over here and tell me what kind you want? We're still getting used to it, but my cooks are the best pizza cooks around." That, I said completely truthfully and didn't bother hiding the pride I felt in my employees.

That got Patricia to smile. "So I've heard from Aaron. Do you think you could ask him to join us?"

She wasn't trying to avoid the other guys. I'd simply already led them past Aaron's table.

"Sure. I'll send Mandy over to get your order, too."

"Thank you, Chris." Martin sounded like he meant it. Maybe they were ready to try again? Christmas had gone terribly wrong, though demon magic had mostly saved the day.

I would always try for Aaron's sake, but I hadn't expected them to lighten up. I got his parents seated, grabbed their drinks, and sent Mandy over with them before heading back to the guys' table and sliding in.

"Hi, beautiful," Aaron said, putting his arm around me.

"You're so full of shit."

He gasped, acting hurt. "No, I'm not. You are beautiful."

His shoulder was warm when I leaned against it, and I rested my head against his firm muscles. Aaron, being a half angel or Nephilim, was super tall.

"Your parents were wondering if you might go join them."

"Sure." He glanced at Brennan and Mal. "Either of you two want to come and save me from them?"

Mal shook his head. "No, thanks. Unless you really need it, then I will."

Brennan nodded with a faint smile, agreeing with Mal's assessment.

"No, I can handle my parents. Way to help a brother out, though." He made a stabbing motion at his heart.

Mal winced. "If it's that bad, I'll come."

"I'll hold down the door," Brennan said.

I scooted out of the booth, grateful I had an excuse to drop in and out of that situation instead of being stuck at the table. Aaron and a reluctant Mal headed over.

Brennan tugged on my hand, and I let him pull me back into the booth with him, surprised when he put his arm around me and tucked me against his side. Brennan had a lot of intimacy issues stemming from a great deal of abuse during his childhood in the fae lands. He was half fae, and they hadn't treated him kindly. His own family had essentially sold him into slavery. I'd helped free him and offered him a place where he could be free to simply exist however he needed to. Brennan was getting more comfortable touching me and being intimate with me. I never pushed him, just offered whatever he wanted while he healed.

"You good?" I tilted my head back so I could meet his gaze with my own.

"Yes, Chris. Thank you." He tucked me against his side, and I took a deep breath.

I hadn't been worried about the opening that much, anyway. My people were pros. But, with everything that had happened, I'd been worried something might go wrong. It seemed that we were doing well, and I let Brennan drag the last bit of tension from me with his touch.

He leaned over and kissed my forehead. "I love you, Chris Price. Thank you for saving me."

"If I recall correctly, you did a great deal of saving as well." I grinned at him, but I knew what he meant. "I love you too, Brennan."

The door chimed again. We both straightened in alarm. We weren't expecting anyone else.

A man and a woman I didn't recognize walked in. The guy wore jeans, and a long-sleeved t-shirt, had dark curly hair and dusky skin. He was solidly built in the way that made me think he either had a very physical job or he worked out. The woman looked similarly strong, and also had dark hair and dark eyes with a lighter skin tone, though she was quite tan.

Brennan studied them closely, but finally shook his head dismissively. Something about them caught my attention, but I couldn't put my finger on what, and a soft brush with my powers revealed nothing.

Shrugging, I reluctantly slid from Brennan's embrace and scooted out of the booth.

"We're not actually open," I said when I came up to them. "How can I help you?"

The man scanned the room while the woman focused on me. "Oh, we heard about this place in a review online and wanted to try it. It looked open. We can come back." She put her hand on the man's arm, and he nodded.

"We are having a training session. The place burned down due to some faulty wiring a while back, and we are reopening in a week. If you're willing to provide constructive feedback, we'll seat you tonight. Food is on the house, just be understanding if the service isn't smooth. All the other customers are regulars who got an invite to the party."

Just then someone shouted out a trivia answer, and another table cheered while others groaned good naturedly.

The couple shared a glance before they shrugged. "Hard to turn down free pizza. That's okay with us."

"Cool, mates. Mandy!"

She was officially moving to a hostess position, though she'd still serve when needed.

Mandy hurried over.

"We have surprise customers. I told them what's up and they're happy for the free food."

Mandy's eyebrows rose, and she nodded. "Thanks for coming in. Booth okay?"

The mystery couple nodded, and Mandy took them to an open booth. I went over to the door and locked it. It'd still let people out, safety and all that, but no one else would wander in.

I shot a glance at Brennan. He gave me a quick smile before glancing down at something, probably a book on his phone. Since he was content, I figured I should go check on Mal and Aaron.

Steeling myself, I headed for their table.

Aaron's parents glanced at me when I sat down next to Mal. He clutched his drink, and tension tightened his shoulders, but he had a reasonably relaxed expression on his face. Maybe he was just nervous? He wasn't especially comfortable with humans knowing he was a vampire, and he was in a room full of people who knew, including Aaron's parents.

Aaron glanced at me and smiled, though his expression remained tight.

"How is the training going, Chris?" Patricia fiddled with her silverware.

"Good. I think they're getting the hang of the wood-fired pizza." At least this was a safe topic.

"It tastes like they are," Martin said before taking another bite of his slice.

Slowly, I relaxed as we made small talk about safe topics, like pizza. I could talk about pizza to almost anyone. The strange encounter in Thailand flickered across my thoughts. I hadn't heard from Lucifer, and I hoped he had everything under control. I didn't really have time to worry about all that with the reopening coming so soon, so

I pushed the thoughts away. I'd worry about them another day.

Dakota Brown

CHAPTER 4

Price

An excited shriek from the kitchen got my attention a short time later.

"Uh, I'd better check on that." I hastily scooted my chair out. Mal also stood, and we hurried for the kitchen.

"What the fuck is that?" I stopped and stared, Mal at my side.

A vaguely human-shaped pillar of flame stood in front of the pizza ovens holding out a twenty to my baffled and terrified employee. This was one of the new folks. Mandy hurried in just after me and stopped, mouth dropping open.

"Chris?" She gasped my name.

"I don't know, mate. Give it a pizza." I shrugged.

"What kind?" Her voice rose. Dating an incubus didn't exactly prepare one for pillars of flame wielding cash.

An approximation of an arm opposite the one holding the twenty pointed to our ingredient list on the wall. He wanted the spicy one. Go figure.

"Yeah, mate, give us twenty minutes." I sighed. We were going to have to tell the new employees everything. Fuck.

Mandy hesitantly took the proffered bill and grabbed Billy from the other room.

"What the fuck?" he breathed.

"Make him a pizza," I ordered, about to do it myself if the rest of the staff couldn't manage. I mean, fair. But still, it wanted a pizza.

Billy stared at me, back at the pillar of flame, and then shook his head. "Yeah, sure. Dustin, you made one of these yet?"

"What?" the new employee squeaked, staring open-mouthed at the sentient flame.

"We're going to make the nice pillar of flame a pizza. It paid. Now, wear two pairs of gloves and don't rub your eyes before you wash your hands. Like this." Billy showed Dustin how to make the spicy pizza, all the while under the watchful eyes of the flame demon—or whatever it was. Pretty sure it was a flame demon. How had it gotten in here, anyway?

The pizza went in the oven. Dustin turned to stare at the creature some more.

"Does this, uh…" he choked. "Does this happen often?"

"Yeah." Billy patted him on the shoulder. "You'll get used to it."

Dustin paled. "For real?"

"For real."

Dustin almost rubbed his face with his gloved hands. Billy caught his arm and tugged him over to the sink. No one wanted chili oil in their eyes.

The pillar seemed to wait patiently while the pizza cooked. Once it had finished, Billy boxed it and handed it to the creature.

It gave the impression of a bow before the floor melted and it sank into the ground, pizza and all.

Before I could start swearing, the floor flowed back into its former state, nothing to show that a flaming supernatural being had just stood there.

"Mal!" I rounded on the vampire.

He held up his hands. "It wanted a pizza. Therefore, it could get through the wards."

I dug my knuckles into my eyes. "'Course it wanted a pizza. The fuck? Where is Sabian?"

"Doing paperwork," Billy said. "It seemed safest. You are used to his aura of sex, and I think everyone who has the pendants is immune, but the new employees aren't."

"Are we going to have to confine him to Mal's occult shop?"

"No. Well. Maybe." Billy shrugged.

Mandy giggled. "He can't help it."

"I know, but it's not exactly fair to the unprotected amongst us." I sighed again. "I'll go see what we can do." Perhaps we could come up with another sort of amulet to protect the employees. We might have to do something regardless. Like Sabian, some supernatural creatures couldn't help how they affected humans.

Mal touched my arm. "Do you want to keep the demons out?"

"Not as much as I want to keep the angels out," I admitted.

Dustin choked again. "Aren't demons worse than angels?"

"Angels are a bunch of assholes. The demons, at least, I can exorcise. Billy, please fill everyone in."

"Right, boss. So, Dustin, got some extra information you should probably know." He gestured, and Dustin followed him back over to the prep counter.

"Shit." I hurried out of the kitchen before I had to deal with Dustin's reactions.

Mal followed, and we went into my office where Sabian stared at the computer.

"Do you need any help?" I asked.

"No. I'm done."

"So, uh, can you not make my staff horny?"

35

Sabian chuckled. "I'm trying. I promise."

"Try harder?"

Sabian turned his charm on me, amber eyes burning with desire. My panties would have combusted if that were possible.

Mal licked his lips before clearing his throat. "Sabian."

"Aww, an incubus has to have some fun sometime."

"Yeah, just not in my office." I was about to jump over the desk and throw myself into Sabian's arms. Or take the closer target and jump the vampire. "Try harder the other way," I muttered, starting to pant.

"Sorry." Sabian managed to look contrite, but I could tell through our bond that he was amused as hell. Sabian's influence had actually been how Mal and I had originally hooked up. I'd rescued Sabian from a cursed amulet and had him trapped in the circle in my basement. He'd been starving and when Mal and I had gone down together to check on him, he'd seen a good opportunity to get fed. I'd already been eyeing the vampire, though I hadn't known he was a vampire at the time, and it really hadn't taken much more than a suggestion from the incubus to get Mal and I together.

I shuddered as the overwhelming need to get laid receded, leaving only a vague need instead. I was used to that, living with Sabian and all. Also, it was not difficult to get laid at my house.

"Tonight?" Sabian grinned at me.

"When we get home, anyway," I agreed before fleeing my office. Mal could deal with Sabian. Incubus was playing dirty tonight.

Screams from the dining area were better than a cold bucket of water to the face. *What now?*

I ran out into the dining area, expecting to have to rebuild the pizza shop again. Instead, I saw a small flock of cherubs darting around the ceiling while the patrons freaked out.

Mal and Sabian met me at the edge of the chaos. "Okay, maybe I should have just kept anything supernatural out," he admitted.

"Too late now. Yo!" I shouted. "They just want a pizza. Chill!"

At the sound of my voice, the cherubs went into a hover, and the guests sat down. Aaron's parents gave me some side-eye, but they didn't say anything as I strode past the table. I crooked my finger at Aaron as I did, and he scrambled out of his chair, following me.

"Find out what they want to eat. Tell them it's on the house tonight for the Michael thing and make sure they don't misbehave." When we'd been trying to bait the archangel Michael into an attack, we'd outright said he was hung like a Cherub. I was still amused by that.

"Sure, Chris."

Mal went with Aaron, and Sabian stayed with me.

I bumped shoulders with him, then set about circulating amongst the tables, calming the patrons.

I used a variation of "they're cherubs, they just want pizza," on everyone and Sabian used a touch of his powers to soothe them, and we basically got the dining area calmed. The surprise guests seemed immune to Sabian's charm, and their level of surprise at the cherubs' presence was different than the rest of my patrons, further setting off some red flags, but I still couldn't find any reason to actually be suspicious.

By the time the angels had their pizza and left, trivia started up again.

"Mal! Come join us! You gotta get the hang of the 80's man," one of my regulars called out. They really enjoyed kicking his ass at trivia.

Mal winked at me as he passed. "I've been studying."

My laugh surprised me, but so far, the night had only been kind of a disaster. The surprise guests weren't terrible, I supposed. It certainly could be worse.

Aaron's parents stared at me, and I artfully—or maybe obviously, I wasn't sure—avoided their table. We'd made some progress. Probably not enough to overcome the supernatural visitors, though. I had no idea how I was going to swing this with the regular patrons, but, hey, there were worse problems to have.

***

Several hours later, I'd managed to get ahold of my own pizza and beer. Brennan was helping the crew clean up, and Dustin had not quit on the spot, but he was pretty wide-eyed. I don't know what Billy had decided to share, but I imagined he'd left some things out. I'd really hoped that the pizza shop could remain out of the picture as far as any further supernatural dealings were concerned. It looked like that wasn't going to happen now.

Aaron had taken off with his parents when they'd left. Most of the patrons had wandered off, and a few of the hardcore regulars were helping to clean up in thanks for the free pizza party. Mal finally joined me.

"Well, did you win?" I grinned at my vampire.

"No, but I gave a good showing for once. They were impressed." He chuckled. "Want to get out of here?" His gaze heated, and I knew exactly what was on his mind.

"Yeah." I stuffed the last of my pizza in my face, finished the beer and waved at my employees.

Brennan and Sabian would know why I'd left. I sent them a quick mental hug through our bond and let Mal put his arm around me as we went through the door. As soon as the door shut behind us, he grabbed my ass.

"Mal, someone might see," I said, mock scandal in my voice.

"And?"

"Okay, point."

Moments later, somehow, I was slung over his shoulder. Damn fast vampire, anyway.

"At least the view is good," I muttered, staring at his ass, and contemplating if I was going to smack him or just enjoy the view.

The Harley-shaped nightstallion revved his engine, as if reminding Mal he was there.

"I haven't forgotten about you, Inferno," Mal said.

I could listen to my vampire talk for hours and not get tired of it. His Arabic accent, softened by a century or more in America, was delicious. Between him and Aaron, I had enough ear candy to last several lifetimes. I'd even listened to Aaron lecture about physics and not gotten bored. One, he was good at explaining things, and two, his voice was every bit as pleasing as Mal's.

My vampire squeezed my leg to warn me, then shifted me off his shoulder. I caught my balance then swung a leg over Inferno the Motorcycle's back.

"Do you mind, Inferno?" Mal asked. The nightstallion usually let my guys ride him, but they were polite and never assumed he would.

The Harley revved again, and Mal swung his leg over the back behind me. He squeezed his thighs around me and put his hands on my waist. I leaned back against his chest as the motorcycle stood itself up and headed for home.

I could ride a motorcycle that didn't have a mind of its own, but sometimes it was nice to let the vehicle drive itself, as it were. Especially when I was riding with a sexy vampire, who had his hands up my shirt.

It took longer than it should have for me to realize we weren't heading toward the house.

"Inferno?" I had to shout over the noise the nightstallion produced as a motorcycle.

Mal nibbled at my neck. I squirmed on the motorcycle seat, Mal's hands cool against my hot skin.

"All part of the plan," he murmured, his voice carried to me magically.

"There's a plan?" My voice slurred, drunk with lust, as Mal slid one hand into my jeans. The vibration of the motorcycle seat, perfectly imitated by the nightstallion combined with Mal's caresses, pulled a moan from my lips.

"Yes," he breathed onto my neck before nipping at me, fangs extended and pressing lightly against my skin before he withdrew.

"Fuck," I gasped with a shudder as Mal slipped his other hand out of my shirt and popped the button on my jeans, giving him better access.

Somewhere along the way, we'd gotten on the interstate. The wind tugged at my hair and beat against my chest, though my eyes and ears were protected through magic, as was my head. I'd asked Inferno to let the wind hit me. Otherwise, it felt strange to ride. He had some pretty epic magical abilities to protect his rider, making it so I didn't require a helmet. Otherwise, I would have worn one.

I'd never gotten finger fucked on a motorcycle at eighty miles an hour before, and it was a damn good thing the nightstallion was driving and protecting me magically because Mal was talented with his fingers. My foot jerked and probably would have killed us if Inferno hadn't been in charge as Mal slipped a finger inside me and curled it, stroking me and sending tremors shivering through my body.

"Come for me, Chris," he whispered against my neck.

40

"Oh gods." I couldn't resist his command and shattered on the back of the motorcycle as we sped down the interstate.

Tremors shivered through me as Mal continued stroking. I hung limp in his arms, all thoughts fleeing as I let myself simply feel: the press of Mal against my back, his finger still inside me, his other hand fondling my breast, the cool wind in my hair contrasting with the lingering warmth rising from the motorcycle.

He held me, stroking me as if idly, something to do with his fingers while he rode. I certainly wasn't hating it, shivers running through me at his touch.

"Since we have a driver, how about you magic away your pants?" he suggested.

"If it's okay with Inferno," I breathed out, head still swimming from the last orgasm. Mal could hear me because of his sensitive ears, and I suspected Inferno blocked the noise more for the vampire than he did me.

The engine revved, and I sensed acceptance through my bond with the nightstallion. He didn't seem bothered by our activities.

The utter ridiculousness of sex on a motorcycle warred with the aching need within me that Sabian had brought to wakefulness at the pizza shop.

"Only if you want to, Chris." Mal's breath tickled my neck.

"I want to."

With that pronouncement, Mal gripped my hips and lifted me so he could slide down onto the primary seat with me in his lap.

A pair of headlights washed over us, reminding me that we weren't alone. I tensed.

"They won't notice." Mal caressed my arms.

"Good. Not into public viewing."

His throaty chuckle sent a special thrill through my body that settled deep inside me, increasing my need.

"How do we do this?"

"You make your pants disappear," he reminded me. "I provide the tool for pleasuring."

"Mate, did you just call your cock a pleasure tool?" I twisted so I could stare at him.

The vampire blinked, then shrugged. "Guess so."

"I'm never going to be able to take it seriously again," I said, deadpan.

"I'm quite certain I can change your mind about that." He nipped at my neck. "Pants. Now."

Concentrating, I focused on my pants leaving my legs and going back to my bedroom. It was something I was working on, and I got it right about half the time.

Mal laughed. "Close enough."

"Well, the important parts are gone." I sighed. Another pair of pants ruined. At least I could fix them pretty well with magic, and if I couldn't, Ezra, my demon prince, could. He was surprisingly good at using magic for domestic chores.

The remains of my jeans sagged around my ankles and stayed buttoned around my waist. I'd made the part between my knees and the waist band vanish. Along with my underwear. I was now speeding down the interstate half naked, and the wind was drying me out.

"Um, Inferno, you could increase the wind protection a tad."

I could almost hear his amused nicker, but the wind cut back a bit.

Mal nibbled at my neck and fingered my clit, stroking me until I was wet again.

"Ready?"

"Might I say once more for the record, this is ridiculous?"

"When's the last time you did something ridiculous that was not life threatening?"

"This isn't life threatening?" I twisted so I could glance at the vampire out of the corner of my eye.

"No. We're on your motorcycle-shaped nightstallion, and he consented to us fooling around. We're about as safe as we could be. It's simply a new position to try."

I relaxed into Mal's arms. He was right, of course.

"I'm ready."

Mal shifted around behind me, freeing his cock from his pants, then slid his finger inside me and stroked, making sure I was ready. Then he lifted me by my hips and lowered me down on his cock.

I didn't try to stop the small cries of pleasure as he filled me, head tilted back, neck instinctively bared for him. He nipped me again, not breaking skin. Goosebumps raced down my skin, and I shivered.

The vibrations of the "engine" combined with Mal's movements, and his hands clamped possessively on my hips, not to mention the sensation of speeding down the interstate, no matter how safe we really were, all heightened the intensity of the moment. I carefully rocked my feet back to the passenger pegs so I could get a little leverage and rode him harder, leaning my hands on unresponsive handlebars. No way was Inferno letting me drive in this state.

Smart.

I squealed as Inferno took a corner fast. Mal held me tight, slamming me down onto him. My pleasure built as Mal thrust into me again, and again. I was crying out now, unable to contain myself.

"Come for me, my exorcist," he ordered, voice rough and full of lust.

If I'd been any less turned on, I might have played with him a little, made him last a bit longer before I managed my own release, but Mal wanted me to come first, and he had to be close himself. I couldn't even imagine how he was holding out, with him getting the full brunt of the vibrations from the bike.

I shouted my release. Mal came with me, slamming me down one last time, before holding me tightly against him. We both trembled from our exertion and the endorphins that raced through us.

Inferno took another fast corner and would have dumped both of us off his back had he not been holding on with his magic.

I finally glanced around, no longer completely occupied by Mal's cock.

Somehow, we'd made it home.

CHAPTER 5

Lucifer

I stared at the man glaring defiantly back at me. Sitting slouched, cheek resting on the palm of my hand and elbow digging into the stone arm of my throne, I wondered why I couldn't have a padded throne. Really, there wasn't any reason I couldn't. Making a mental note to redecorate, I tried to focus on my task. Redecorating was way more interesting than torturing the shithead who had attacked me and Chris.

Which was a little weird. Even I had to admit that.

"Boss?"

"Yes, Taus?" Relieved to have something to distract me, I turned to one of my high-level demons.

You might call Taus something of an administrator. He handled a lot of the day-to-day things in Hell. Especially when I was away, and as much as I trusted any demon, I trusted Taus. There were only two demons I trusted more, and that was because they were bound to Chris, and she'd have all sorts of things to say if either Ezra or Sabian betrayed me. Of course, if I betrayed them, well, I wouldn't bet on myself over Chris Price. She'd hand my ass to me. Not that I'd tell anyone that, of course.

"Can I have a word?"

My captive wasn't going anywhere. Magical chains bound him to the floor, so I heaved myself to my feet and followed the demon to the back of the dais where my throne sat and through a thick stone door.

Taus wasn't particularly impressive in appearance. He was tall, had coal black skin, cloven hooves, muscles I was sure Chris would appreciate aesthetically, and a long tail with a tuft of black hair at the end. Broad shoulders supported a head with impressive bull horns on top. All of our doorways were wider than a human's for his comfort. But demons that looked like him were so common, down here he wasn't impressive. On Earth, maybe.

"Boss. We got a problem." His normally granite-on-granite voice was even more grumbly and grave than normal.

"What now?" I sighed, not even sure what I expected.

"There are concerns." Taus glanced away and twisted his hands together as if he were nervous. He knew I wasn't the sort to punish the messenger, so this had to be terrible. Like worse than the imp uprising several hundred years ago. On the whole, imps weren't dangerous, however enough of them could be a problem for anyone. Fortunately, they weren't very good at working together.

"Taus, just tell me."

He took a deep breath before blurting. "Some of the demons think you are becoming too tame."

"Too tame?" That certainly wasn't what I had expected.

"When's the last time you tortured someone?"

I blinked, trying to think. "I'm not sure I've had an occasion to even consider it recently."

"What about that human in the throne room? Why isn't he screaming out his every sin?"

I stared at Taus. Could he be right?

"We, uh, talked. And, uh, we think you need to up your game, as it were." He glanced away then back at me. "Boss," he added respectfully.

"And what do you propose I do?" If he suggested giving up Chris, I was going to paint the walls with someone's blood.

"I have a list of demons whose transgressions warrant higher level attention. Maybe make some examples. The human in there? Make him scream. You're the devil. Act like it."

The last he said a little defiantly.

I ran a hand through my hair, then glanced back toward the human in the throne room.

"I am not quite sure I see where this is coming from. Did we not just fight off a major coup attempt?"

"The exorcist did most of that, begging your pardon. The talk was that while she was briefly in control of Hell, things were starting to feel more like normal again. Then you returned and everything got, well, dull. She's the best thing that's happened to this realm in a while. Again, begging your pardon. No one wants to overthrow you. Don't worry on that account. Well, I mean, no more than the normal scheming and what not. We are demons, after all. But, if you don't do something, someone will start getting ideas. Mammon's little insurrection wasn't so out of the abyss as you might imagine."

"Wait, you're not upset about Chris?"

"The exorcist is the best thing that has happened to Hell in ages. As I said. I realize that's strange. We're demons. We need conflict. Everyone likes her. Some of them are so excited to face her in combat, they're training. Can you imagine that? Demons training?"

I stood in alarm. "Is she in danger?"

"It's Hell. Of course, she's in danger. She also knows that. You, perhaps, have gotten complacent."

Perhaps the dichotomy of demons loving my exorcist so much they were training to fight her wouldn't make sense to a human, but it made a lot of sense to me. I'd have to warn her she'd made such a favorable impression that she was going to get challenged soon.

"Very well." I tapped my foot, thinking. "I will attempt to be less complacent and more like Chris. You may have to advise me, as it appears I have sunken into bad patterns."

Taus took a deep breath. "Yes, boss. Start with that human. We need to know why he attacked you and the exorcist."

"I can think of a lot of reasons." I shrugged. "But yes, let's go find out."

***

Hours later, I had a lot of interesting information, and Brady was a gibbering pile of mental goo on the floor of the throne room. Taus was searching for an appropriate place in Hell to toss one of "God's Warriors." This man had more innocent blood on his hands than many of the criminals that ended up down here. It seemed that the darker parts of the Christian church were up to their old, evil tricks.

Brady was part of the inquisition. And his primary target was Chris.

This, honestly, wasn't surprising. It was, however, extremely annoying. I wasn't worried about Chris's safety. Not from simple humans, anyway. Though this man had claimed the true faith and called on it to protect him, that sort of Godly power only worked for people who were truly Godly. Not folks who used God's name to justify killing or other crimes.

I shook my head and watched as a few lesser demons squirmed their way across the floor, cleaning up the blood and excrement.

"Boss?"

"Yes, Taus?"

"That was a start. What do we do about the inquisition?"

After a moment's consideration, I smiled. "Maybe we should send out some hunters of our own."

The bull-headed demon grinned grotesquely. "I'll summon them."

CHAPTER 6

Price

Something pulled me from a deep sleep. My eyes snapped open, and I listened. Nothing.

Grumbling, I tried to roll over, but since I was piled in between Sabian and Mal, I couldn't.

Mal's breathing shifted. I'd woken him. He was a light sleeper. Though Mal didn't have to breathe, since he was a vampire, he had taught his body to keep the habit because otherwise people got all freaked out about it. Sabian was not a light sleeper. I could have probably dropped hellfire on him and he might have slept through it.

The bedroom door creaked and the heavy sound of Mayhem's paws padding across the carpet eased me. But only for a moment. If he was in hellhound form, something had to be going on.

The sound came again, closer this time. It was my phone, and the screen lit up in Mayhem's mouth as he brought it to me. I must have left it in another part of the house.

If it hadn't been Billy's ringtone, I would have ignored it even with the hellhound bringing me the device. The last few weeks since we'd officially opened had been quiet, and I supposed it was about time for something to go wrong. My manager wouldn't bother me unless it was important, and I held out my hand. The hellhound dropped the phone into my hand, and I wrinkled my lips before casting a quick cleaning spell to get the drool off. Handy, that.

I didn't even look at the clock, though I didn't think I'd been asleep that long.

"S'up, mate?" I slurred.

"Chris, I'm so sorry to bother you, but, uh, my sister has gotten herself into a situation and, well, we need an exorcist."

"The fuck?" That cleared the cobwebs from my brain.

Sabian grumbled as I sat up, dislodging his heavy arm from where it had lain across my stomach.

Mal touched my shoulder, letting me know he was there.

"That's what *I* said when she called. She's babysitting and, well, there was a lot of screaming. I'm getting the impression demons are involved."

"Shit!" I scrambled out of bed, cast another cleaning spell over myself since I could, and hurriedly pulled on clothing.

Mal was already dressed and heading for the door by the time I stomped my feet into my boots.

"I'll text you the address."

"Thanks. Mal and I are on our way."

Billy hung up, and I ran for the door. Mal handed me a bag, and I glanced through it before slinging it over my shoulder and going out into the cool desert evening. Inferno waited, pawing the ground, flaming tail swishing. He presented his back, as if he already knew what was going on and in moments, Mal and I were astride. Mayhem flew alongside as we took the crow's path to the address Billy had sent. I didn't recognize the address from Billy's paperwork at the pizza shop, so I didn't think this was where he lived. Maybe his family home?

When we arrived and Inferno shifted into a motorcycle to avoid notice, we found ourselves in a quiet middle-class suburban neighborhood. The house was a modest two-level home, and I knew we were in the right spot because Billy's car was in the driveway, along with another I didn't recognize.

I even felt the hint of demonic energy. My ability to sense it was way stronger now that I had a demon mark—and hopefully two again soon. If you'd have told me a year ago that I'd be calmly walking into a situation involving demons with no hint of fear or worry, I'd have laughed in your face.

Mal carried our bag of tools in case we needed them. Chances were, we wouldn't. Demons just listened to me these days. How weird was that?

I didn't even have to knock. A white-faced Billy opened the door when we got close. He must have been watching.

"I don't even know if I should be laughing, or terrified right now," he admitted.

I took a breath and gestured for him to let us in.

A teen that looked like a younger, feminine version of Billy stood in front of three kids, maybe ranging from six to ten, and two kobolds. Knobby, animalistic, almost doggish demons that were clearly not the problem because Billy's sister was apparently protecting them, too.

I turned to where their gaze was fixed and raised my eyebrows.

"Seriously?"

Billy shrugged a little helplessly. "Not ours. Sis is babysitting."

On the floor in front of the fireplace was a rug. A rug with a summoning board as the design. Once upon a time I would have marveled at the stupidity of someone having anything like that in their house, and a quiet trickle of fear would have wormed its way through me as I tried to figure out how to deal with the situation. Now I'd literally been to

Hell, and a summoning board really wasn't a huge deal. Of course, it still could be dangerous to others, so I took it seriously. Just, uh, the robot vacuum frantically whirring around on top of it, caught on an unraveled string of carpet, was kind of ruining the seriousness of the moment.

"Who runs a vacuum bot in the middle of the night?" I finally blurted out.

"We were showing Jazzy," one of the girls said nervously. "She's never seen how good they work."

I glanced at Billy's sister, guessing she was Jazzy. The teen shrugged, looking a little chagrined.

"And what the hell are you two doing here?" I pointed at the kobolds.

They freaking bowed.

"Apologies, mistress. We were summoned."

"By that?" I gestured at the bot.

They nodded.

"Are you now bound to obey the bot?" I managed to keep a straight face when I said it, but only barely.

The kobolds drooped, their long ears flopping when they nodded.

"Seriously?" Okay, they weren't the brightest creatures, either.

"Mistress, if you send us home, the bond will be broken."

"For Christ's sake, go home," I commanded.

They winced at the religious profanity, then poofed out of existence. And that was why I was no longer frightened by simple demon encounters. Most of them did what I told them without theatrics.

The girls' eyes all widened, and even Billy looked a little surprised.

I returned my attention to the summoning rug and the bot. The demonic energy was gone, but something was still off. Mal sensed it, too. He put out a hand in caution when I took a step toward the robot.

"Yeah, I feel it," I assured him. "Show yourself," I commanded.

Icy laughter echoed around the room. "You may have command of the demons," it said. "But I do not have to do as you say."

A greenish glow started in the fireplace.

"Great," I muttered as the girls all squealed in fear.

"What is it?" Billy came over to stand with his sister.

"Some sort of ghost." I wrinkled my lips, thinking.

"Ghosts are real, too?" Billy squeaked out.

"Yeah, mate. Ghosts are real." I sighed. I really hated dealing with ghosts. It had been a long time since I'd had to, as well. Though I'd dealt with a lot of demons over the last few months, the last ghost I'd dealt with had been years ago before I quit being an exorcist and retired to run the family pizza shop.

Mayhem sauntered into the room, eliciting more squeals of fear, which he ignored. The flames glowing in his eyes flared as he snagged the bot in his teeth and ripped it away from the summoning board and the piece of carpet that had entangled it. The bot beeped in alarm, crying about having fallen off a cliff while the ghost howled in rage. Mayhem lashed his head back and forth, and the bot fell silent. Those things weren't cheap. I hoped the hellhound hadn't melted it.

"The way is open," it hissed. "More come."

"Well, we're going to close the f—"

Billy cleared his throat.

Right. Kids.

"We're going to close the way and send you home. Wouldn't you like to go home?" I tried for a civil voice.

It howled again, and we all winced.

55

"Would have been nice if it were that easy," I muttered.

Mal shrugged. "So we banish the ghost. Shouldn't be too hard. Billy, why don't you get the kids out of here?"

Just then, two adults walked into the house. A man and a woman, probably mid-thirties, dressed like they'd been out on a date night. Probably the kids' parents or guardians. They stopped and stared at me just long enough to form the question of who the hell we were, but not actually utter it, before the ghost screamed out of the fireplace, splattering ectoplasm everywhere and slamming into the woman.

"Fuck." I tossed the bag of tools at Mal. He was faster than I was and should know what to do. We needed to banish that ghost.

Mayhem tossed the bot aside and breathed hellfire on the rug just as it glowed green.

"Wait!" I shouted, too late. It was all I could do to cast a spell in time to keep the hellfire from burning through the floor and setting the entire house ablaze. The situation was not so dire that we needed to nuke the entire house.

Children screamed. The man shouted. Billy dragged his sister and the kids out of the house. I thought about joining them, just as Mal called out the first words of a banishment.

"Hey!" I waved my hands at the possessed woman, trying to distract the ghost.

She levitated, emitting a banshee scream. Mal clapped his hands over his ears, breaking off the incantation.

"Bitch," I muttered, and hit her with a fist-sized ball of energy straight to the diaphragm. Not enough to hurt her, just enough to knock the wind out of her, hoping to get her to stop shrieking.

It worked so well the ghost screamed out of the woman and flew straight at me, splattering green goo everywhere.

I threw up a shield and ducked in time to avoid tangling directly with the specter. She slammed into the wall behind me and vanished, leaving behind a splash of ectoplasm.

For a moment, everything was quiet.

The man had helped the woman sit up, and they stared at me, dazed. The man's gaze flicked toward Mayhem when he moved to my side, but otherwise didn't seem to register the hellhound.

Wordlessly, I moved to Mal's side where he was sprinkling a salt circle on their carpet. While I'd never consider using a carpeted surface for a demon, between Mal and I, we should have enough power to hold a ghost long enough for one of us to banish it. We just had to get it to stay still for a few minutes.

Mal made some designs in the salt and lit an orange candle in the middle. I was pretty sure that was from a Halloween decoration. Right now it would work well enough for the purpose.

I glanced at his work out of habit. Mal had so much more formal training than I did, it was more likely I'd make a mistake than him. Still, it didn't hurt. Mal held his ritual knife and intoned a summoning in a language I didn't know. Probably something from his younger years long enough ago that even I hadn't come across it.

The ghost responded immediately. Either the language was potent, or the specter was simply happy to oblige. The glowing shape swooped into the salt circle and Mal blew out the candle. Almost visible lines of energy arched up from the salt circle, trapping the ghost.

Well, that was more powerful than I'd expected. Especially from a circle on carpet.

The ghost floated there, ragged hair dancing around her head as if in zero gravity, her tattered dress fluttering in an invisible breeze; her face a nearly skeletal mask with sunken eye sockets and glowing green orbs where eyes would have been.

At first, I thought maybe she was simply accepting our help to send her home. After a moment of quiescence she wailed. Mal must have planned for this, because the energy containing her filtered the sound down to a tolerable level. Rage twisted her features, and she threw herself at the invisible barrier.

Mal again uttered the words that would banish her back to wherever she had come from, but the ghost had one last trick. She flicked her fingers toward the remains of the rug that she had come through. Despite it being melted into plastic slag by my hellhound, a portal snapped open and green light streamed out.

"Mayhem, wait!" I shouted as the hellhound bounded gleefully forward.

Grumbling, the creature backed off, and I cast a shield, catching a few specters before they could escape. Through our bond, I could feel Mayhem's desire to pounce on the ghosts and tear them apart. Perhaps he thought they were fun toys. I simply shoved them back through the portal and used my magic to snap it closed while Mal finished banishing our ghost.

I turned in time to see her barf ectoplasm all over the floor in one last attempt to free herself from the salt circle. It might have worked, too, but Mal shouted the last words of the ritual, and she vanished in an explosion of goo. Unfortunately, the circle vanished at the same time and the slime coated everything. And I do mean everything.

Have I mentioned how much I hated ghosts?

"Ew." I flicked my hands, trying to shake off the nasty shit.

"What just happened?" the man demanded, breaking the awkward silence that followed my exclamation of distaste.

"Daddy!" One of the girls ran back into the house and into her dad's arms. She immediately shrieked in dismay as she got slimed.

Billy and his sister and the other kid followed more slowly.

"Looks like your poor choice of décor combined with your robot vacuum called a ghost," I said. "But your babysitter was smart and called the ghost exterminators." I gestured at myself and Mal. "We've got you covered. No need for alarm."

On that note, I frantically gestured for Mal to leave and hurried out of the house.

"Ghost exterminators?" he murmured once we were out of the house.

"I mean, ghost busters might have triggered some red flags." I shrugged. "As long as they leave us alone, I don't care what they think about it later when they have a minute to speak."

Mal chuckled. "So, want to do that handy cleaning spell so we can get out of here?"

"Best idea all day." I muttered the spell and... nothing happened. "What the fuck?" I snarled and tried it again.

Inferno nickered in amusement.

"Laugh all you want, buddy. You're our ride home."

That shut him up.

Mayhem stared at me, opening his mouth as if offering to spray us down with hellfire.

"I don't think that will work the way you intend it to, Mayhem," I countered with a sigh. "I've never been slimed like this before, but it honestly doesn't surprise me that my spell isn't working. That would just be too easy."

Billy came over after helping his sister into her car. She sped away. I didn't blame her.

"So, uh, that was gross." He tried to wipe some of the ectoplasm off.

"Yeah, try salt water when you get home," I offered.

"I will. Thanks for coming, Chris. I'm not sure what we would have done otherwise."

"Of course, Billy. Now get out of here. You have an early morning tomorrow."

He groaned. "Don't remind me."

I laughed as he walked away. "Salt water!" I called after him.

"My poor car," I heard him moan, before he got in and left.

Inferno snorted when we came closer. He shook his head and stomped.

"Yeah, okay, portal then?"

He nodded, sending his flaming mane dancing around him.

Mal stared into the distance, staying quiet. Only the sounds of yelling from inside the now ghost-free house and a car motor rumbling down the street broke the stillness.

"What's up, mate?"

"I don't know. I feel like someone is watching us. I don't actually see anything, though."

"Not sure if there's anything we can do about it unless they show themselves." I hoped my portal-making skills were up to the task of getting us home.

"It's simply odd that someone might be watching us that caught my attention," Mal persisted. "A normal human probably wouldn't have."

"You're right. Do you want to investigate?"

After another extended silence, Mal shook his head. "No, let's go home."

"Okay." I pulled on my magic, intent on making a portal.

I did get one to open. That was a plus.

"You are coming with us," I said to Inferno. "Just in case this doesn't go where I think it does."

He snorted but didn't otherwise protest.

Mal grimaced and took my hand and followed me into the portal, Mayhem at our side and Inferno on our heels.

CHAPTER 7

Mandy

I licked my lips in trepidation and stared at the keys in my hand and the brand-new hybrid Chris had bought for the shop. This had been my idea, but it didn't mean I was comfortable with it. I'd never done any sort of delivery driving before, and houses could be really hard to find, even with GPS. Technically, I was now a hostess. But our business had expanded with the addition of the supernatural clients, and I'd suggested delivery. Chris had been willing to give it a try, so here I was, giving it a try.

Ugh.

It was also late. And brief memories of my kidnapping flashed through my mind. I had Mal on speed dial, but still. I had all of Chris's guys on speed dial. Most of us at the shop did at this point. Even better, I had Warrick. My incubus boyfriend, given to me by Lucifer, peered over my shoulder. Given wasn't the right word, but it also was. Warrick and I both had a choice in the matter, but so far, we were exceptionally pleased with the situation.

Warrick stood behind me.

"Mandy, my love, you can get someone else to do this." His low voice was like smooth velvet caressing my body.

"It was my idea, Warrick. I've just never done anything like this before."

"I'll be with you." He grinned.

"You've never done anything like this, either."

His low chuckle did things to me that were certainly inappropriate for work.

"No, but at least you won't be alone. Let's do this. This is all experimental anyway. If it goes badly, we'll just comp the customer and figure out where we went wrong." He picked up the pizzas from the warmer and gestured for the door.

Warrick had an elegance in his motion that reminded me of a dancer or something elven from a movie. Every motion was graceful, and wow, did that translate nicely to the bedroom.

Jerking my thoughts away from that and ignoring Warrick's knowing smirk, I headed for the door.

Warrick didn't technically work for the pizza shop, but Chris had approved of him riding along with me while making deliveries. We all knew some of my customers wouldn't be human, and having a demon along, even an incubus, was reasonable protection. Warrick was still trying to figure out what he wanted to do up here, besides being a fantastic boyfriend. He'd taken some direction from Sabian and was making himself useful by cleaning and cooking. Honestly, that was enough for me. I was just happy as hell not to be alone, and Warrick was a fantastic house mate.

I was also really glad to have company tonight. Since the pizza shop had reopened a couple of weeks ago, we'd had all sorts of interesting patrons. I honestly kind of enjoyed the change.

Chris knew that normally the delivery drivers used their own vehicles, but she'd felt better with us using a company car. Especially considering some of our clientele. Gabriel had made good on their word to let everyone know our pizza was good, and the rest of the staff had almost gotten used to the random otherworldly customers that showed up occasionally. They didn't always understand the concept of money. Chris had told everyone not to argue overly much and that if they couldn't pay, the rules of the supernatural dictated they'd owe us something in the future. She had started a separate list for any supernatural customer who was short just so we could keep track for the books.

"Mandy, love." Warrick kissed my shoulder. "The pizzas will get cold."

I nodded, stopped procrastinating, and got into the hybrid. Warrick folded into the passenger seat. I popped the address into the GPS and off we went.

The address wasn't too far, and I pulled into the neighborhood. It was a nicer one with large houses.

Even if the GPS hadn't directed me true, it would have been pretty obvious which house the large order of pizzas was going to. Cars lined the streets in front of a huge house with lights on and music spilling out. Party time, clearly.

I found the closest open parking space and got out. We split the load of pizzas and headed for the door, Warrick trailing behind me.

When I rang, a woman opened the door, beer in a red plastic cup sloshing over the side as she listed slightly. She was wearing a cute black party dress and had a cheap sparkly tiara on her head.

"Pizza guy!" she shouted, despite my obvious "not guy" appearance.

I didn't take offence, just offered her my stack of pies. They'd already paid, so I just needed to hand them over.

"Who's got the tip!" she shouted over her shoulder.

"Katie!" another woman shouted.

"Wait here." She went into the house with her stack of pies.

Before my incubus could hand over his pile, a couple of similarly dressed and tiaraed women grabbed his arms and dragged him inside.

"Pizza guy brought the stripper too!" one of the girls shouted.

Warrick glanced over his shoulder at me, eyes wide, as if wondering what to do.

I stared for a moment, not having expected to have to be the rescuer as he was pulled farther into the house.

The first woman shoved some cash at me and shut the door in my face.

"Uh." I held up my hand to protest, too late. I tried the handle. It was locked, and no one answered the doorbell.

They were going to eat Warrick alive.

Well, he was an incubus. I was sure he could handle himself and get a snack at the same time, but did I just leave him here?

I had no idea what to do, so I pulled out my phone.

CHAPTER 8

Price

My phone rang just as I stepped into the portal. Hopefully, I'd be able to call back whoever it was once I was on the other side. I felt a weird tug, just as the portal snapped shut well before it should have, cutting off Inferno. My ears popped as the portal closed and I stumbled, disoriented.

Mayhem roared just as Mal grabbed me and jerked me to the side. A blue light flashed through the blackness, slamming into the hellhound. He absorbed the energy, his internal fires glowing brightly as he used it to charge up.

Something cool and wet with a slightly flowery scent splashed over us, mixing with the ectoplasm and making me feel even grosser. Mayhem yelped, more startled than hurt based on his tone and the feeling through our bond. I threw out a bit of power, trying for light. Magic relating to demons, exorcisms, and wards, I was pretty good at. Everything else was hit or miss. Though I was getting better.

Mal hissed as the room went from dark to daylight bright.

"Fuck," I muttered and hastily attempted to drop the light level.

The vampire wasn't the only one upset about the sudden change in illumination. Once I'd blinked my vision

67

clear, I made out four other people rubbing at their eyes. They quickly recovered, though the other thing I noticed a bit more slowly was the crossbows leveled at us. Despite my mistake with the light, their aim hadn't wavered.

I threw myself in front of Mal, and Mayhem crouched next to me, ready to spring. A low growl rumbled from his throat.

We were in some sort of cellar. The floor was uneven concrete, and the walls were cinderblock. There wasn't much down here, but a flare of power that rose around us caught my attention. It felt a little like the inside of one of my demon traps, only with a different flavor to the magic. It might hold Mayhem, though his bond to me gave him a lot of leeway when it came to things like this. It shouldn't bother me, or Mal.

Mal stood behind me, his hands on my waist as he let me, and my absurdly powerful wards, protect him from the crossbows in front of us.

Two of the people looked vaguely familiar. Had I seen them at the pizza shop not long ago? The familiar woman had dark eyes and dark hair with lighter skin. The guy had dusky skin like Mal's and dark, curly hair. The other two, another man and a woman, were also dark-haired and dark eyed. The man had short-cropped hair and swarthy skin. The woman was fairly pale.

"Uh, hello?" I finally broke the silence after the four of them continued to stare.

The woman on the right stared at the pewter pitcher she held and frowned before glancing back at us.

I risked a look around. The only exit was through them, and I wasn't about to try another portal if they could jerk us off course so easily. I wondered how they'd managed that. Actually, I really wanted to know.

"So, how'd you pull that off, mate? I didn't even know it was possible to redirect a portal." I sauntered forward, casually stepping over the edge of the spell and scuffing the design they'd made on the floor with chalk.

Their eyes widened though they held their ground, shifting the aim of their crossbows as I moved. Mal kept close behind me.

"I gotta warn you, hitting me with projectiles is a terrible idea." I held up my arm to show some of the sigils. "Wards. They'll send anything you send toward me back at you."

"If you're so powerful, how'd you end up his thrall?" The man I didn't recognize pointed at Mal.

I blinked a few times as I processed his words before I burst out laughing. "What the fuck?"

"You heard me."

I laughed harder, wiping tears and ghost goo from my eyes. "Who the hell are you folks?"

"Chris, I think they're serious." Mal squeezed my arm in warning.

"No shit, Mal, just, this is hilarious. Give me a minute." I wasn't sure why I thought this was so funny. Maybe it was Mal's proclivities toward kinky bedroom games contrasting with his general willingness to let me take the lead otherwise.

"This isn't funny," another one of them insisted, though I wasn't sure which one.

"Oh, it is." I finally got myself under control. "Seriously though, who are you, and how did you grab my portal?"

"We are hunters." This woman had a faint accent I couldn't place.

"Hunters?" I glanced back at Mal. He shook his head, not knowing what they were talking about either apparently.

"We used a spell to redirect your portal. Now, if you are not his thrall, perhaps you are unaware of his depredations."

This brought me back to near tears of laughter, again thinking of our bedroom games. Totally inappropriate, but hell, I'd faced down powerful demons and angels. A handful of hunters didn't scare me much. Not that I intended to underestimate them, of course. Just, I wasn't getting the feeling they were much of a threat to me personally. Mal? Maybe.

Mayhem huffed and sat next to me.

The hunters got a little wide-eyed whenever they looked at him but didn't otherwise act surprised. Interesting.

"Mal is relatively harmless." I poked the vampire, as if to demonstrate. "Not that he's not dangerous, but he's pretty mellow until provoked."

"What is it that you think I've done?" Mal's melodic accent washed through me, grounding me a bit.

"Infecting entire cities with thralls just waiting for the time to be right to take control of governments and the world," the chatty man hissed angrily.

I glanced at Mal again. "You've been busy."

He tightened his lips before speaking. "Chris, what do you think the chances are that you released a vampire when you broke the Vatican's prison?"

"Fuck if I know, Mal. I was trying to rescue Ezra. The pope isn't interested in sharing any information about what we let loose, and I'm not sure if anyone else we know has a list." The only person who might was Lucifer. I didn't think bringing him up right then was the best idea. "Why?"

"Because that sounds vaguely familiar. Not anyone I ever met, but an ancient story about an insane vampire who had especially terrible powers. The stories don't even agree that he really was a vampire since his powers were so unusual and terrible. Some think he was a demon." Mal's voice flattened with worry.

"Oh. Huh. Well, that's a problem, now isn't it?" I sobered. "Freaking can't even get a couple of months off between apocalypses? I guess if he is a demon, it'll be easier to deal with than if he's a vampire, though." The bright side, right? Of course, the way our luck ran, this asshole was definitely a vampire.

Mal tightened his hands on my waist but didn't otherwise answer.

The four hunters traded glances.

"Explain," one of the women demanded.

"So, this demon named Mammon—"

They all jerked back as if I'd shocked them. "You should not mention a demon's name. They might decide to take interest." The woman glared at me.

"Oh, he's really extremely dead, so I wouldn't worry." I waved away their concern, to their astonished expressions. "Mal even knows his true name."

The vampire nodded at their incredulous expression.

"Anyway, Asshole decided he wanted to take over Hell, and the best way to do that was to start an apocalypse. Well, *the* Apocalypse, actually. I guess he tried twice. I got involved the second time. Certain individuals in Heaven wanted it, too, and they teamed up, if you can believe it. We"—I gestured at Mal—"and a few of our friends stopped them."

I waited while they absorbed that information before continuing, tapping my foot impatiently. "Anyway, Mal hasn't been out of my sight for more than a day or two at the most since we met. Hardly enough time for him to create cities of minions."

The hunters finally lowered their crossbows, probably figuring they no longer had the drop on us and that I wasn't lying about my wards, or that we were telling the truth and not who they were looking for.

"Why are you covered in goo?" One of the women finally asked a question I probably should have gotten sooner.

"We tangled with a ghost. One of my employee's sisters had a babysitting gig go badly." I shrugged. "We were heading home to clean up. So, where are we?" I took another glance around, but there were no clues other than that the air was relatively dry and cool.

"Not too far from your pizza parlor." They didn't offer any further information.

"Well, I'm Chris Price. You know that. This is Malak Naji, and this magnificent beast is Mayhem."

The hellhound growled softly at the hunters.

"You travel in strange company for an exorcist, Chris Price," one of the men said.

"Yeah, well, you get used to it." I shrugged, not interested in their opinions of my mates. "So, you're looking for this demon or vampire? Want to tell us about it?"

They shared a moment of silent communication before they all stepped back, giving Mal and me some space.

"I am Asher, this is Becca, Perl, and Gael. We've been tracking a vampire for months now. We know it's male, old, and depraved."

"Gathered that already." I gestured for them to continue, ignoring their annoyed glares.

"It seems to have come this direction, but we're not sure how many it has infected on the way."

Mal's fingers tightened on my waist again. He still stood behind me, and I could almost hear him thinking about being pissed off that more people knew what he was. Or maybe I was simply feeling the emotion through our bond.

"That's all we know."

I didn't believe them, but really, I didn't expect more than that.

"Vampires are no joke. Do you really think you are prepared to fight one? Especially one that sounds like he's off his rocker?" I really wanted to know how they thought they were going to take on a supernatural being like a powerful vampire.

They stared back at me, remaining silent.

"Cool. Well, me and Mal, we need to get back before the rest of the team comes looking for us. No one wants that." I wasn't sure if anyone knew we were technically missing yet, but Inferno had to be upset if nothing else, and I imagined it wouldn't be long before he came crashing through the door.

A loud thud sounded from somewhere else in the structure.

"Ahh, too late. Probably Inferno."

"It is," Mal confirmed.

"Leave. Control your demons. Pray we don't see you again." Gael's glare could have peeled paint.

Sighing, I pushed past the hunters, who backed away as we went by, and hurried up the stairs to stop Inferno from bringing the structure down in flames.

We intercepted the nightstallion before it got too bad, and this time he let us climb aboard despite the hardening goo that still coated us.

"Sorry, buddy." I patted his neck and his skin shivered under my touch, though he only snorted and launched us into the sky and toward home.

Belatedly, I remembered that my phone had rung right before we stepped into the portal.

As soon as we touched down at the house, I pulled out my phone and checked the screen. Mandy. Uh-oh. She was delivering tonight. I'd hoped to have a chance to clean up before I had to head back out. At least Brennan and Sabian had made it home, if the car in the driveway was any indication.

I wiped my hands off on my pants and unlocked the phone before returning her call. It rang. And rang.

Finally, just when I was about to panic, she answered.

"Chris, I don't know what to do. They have Warrick."

"Who?" I glanced at Mal, who listened intently, standing next to Inferno.

"The bachelorettes. They think he's the stripper. The door is locked. How do I get him back?"

"Uh." I was not even remotely prepared for that sort of problem. "Well, they probably won't hurt him—"

"Billy is finally calling me back. Hold on."

The line went quiet, and I turned my attention to Mal.

"What the actual fuck?"

He had the audacity to smile. "Warrick is probably fine."

"I'm sure he's more than fine, but…"

Sabian and Brennan came out to check on us and we filled them in.

Sabian snorted in amusement. "I wonder if they actually had a stripper lined up, or just reacted to Warrick's energy."

"I think we need to save him." I sighed, ready for my own bed.

"How about Brennan and I take care of it?" Sabian offered, a mischievous smile lighting up his face.

"That sounds amazing." More than happy to let the guys handle the situation, I headed for the house.

"Besides, Ezra stopped by." Sabian made it seem like an afterthought.

That perked me right up. "He'd better still be here." I glanced back at the incubus, but just thinking about my demon prince gave me a sense of him through our shared mark. He was still here.

Sabian winked. Mal held up the keys to his car and gestured to it. "How about I drive?"

"How about you get clean first," Brennan insisted, wrinkling his nose and waving his hand. Unlike my magic, his worked and Mal was no longer covered in ectoplasm.

Inferno snorted, stamping his paw and tossing his head.

Brennan obliged, getting the ectoplasm off the nightstallion too.

"Are you going to make me beg?" I demanded next.

Brennan turned. "Of course not. Though Ezra could help you as well."

"Please, just get this crap off me."

The mage chuckled, and the tingle of his energy washed over me.

"Thank fuck." I shuddered, and tugged on the Price's Pizza Parlor shirt I wore under my leather jacket. "I really hate dealing with ghosts."

"I'll fill you in," Mal offered at Brennan's questioning glance.

I turned and practically sprinted for the door. I hadn't seen Ezra in far too long. It had been at least a week.

CHAPTER 9

Sabian

"So, how do we go about doing this?" I had lots of ideas, but I wasn't sure what the others were up for.

Mal finished his call to Mandy, getting the address and telling her we were on our way.

"How do you want to do it? We can simply walk in the front door," Brennan said, from the backseat. "Or we can try to extract him more creatively."

Mal chuckled. "Are you hungry, Sabian?" The vampire shoved the car into reverse and backed out of the driveway.

"Always. Well, not actually, but kind of." I hoped that would make sense. I was always sated these days, but that didn't mean I couldn't go for a snack. I fiddled with the seatbelt strap while Mal drove.

Mal sighed. "I'm not going to take my clothes off, but you certainly can."

"Do you think Chris would mind?" I hadn't done a good strip tease in forever. Even for Chris. I made a mental note to work one of those in soon.

"No," both Mal and Brennan said at once.

"But Mandy might not be ready to share Warrick in that way, and a house full of drunk women could be tricky. He might also not have enough practice handling that sort of situation. You can distract them while we get Warrick out," Mal continued.

"I'll just make sure they follow the hands-off rules, and we'll be good then," I said, a little more confidently than I felt.

Mal clapped his hand on my shoulder. "You'll be fine."

It didn't take long for us to find Mandy. She stood by the pizza shop car wringing her hands.

"What do we do?" She asked when we pulled up and got out of the car.

Mal got out and put an arm around her. "Everything will be fine, Mandy. They aren't going to hurt him. He probably just doesn't know how to extract himself."

Mandy snorted. "I'm sure he's fine. I just don't want to leave him, and I panicked a little. Sorry."

"No need to apologize, Mandy. You got dragged into this world because of us. We're happy to help you navigate it."

Mandy visibly melted at Mal's reassurance. Her energy relaxed. It wasn't so much that she loved Mal, more that she trusted him so completely it was a type of love. Not romantic, but still powerful. She remained in his embrace, comforted by his touch.

"Now, I want you to stay in the car and wait. Brennan is going to unlock the door for us and then come wait with you. Sabian and I will deal with the horny women." Mal guided her to his car and sat her down in the passenger seat while she snorted again.

I wondered why Mal wasn't unlocking the door. I knew he had all sorts of vampire powers he never used, though he hadn't said why.

Brennan unlocked the door, and Mal and I entered the large house. The music was loud enough to be uncomfortable for me. The vampire had to be hating it, but he made no complaints, just headed in the direction we both sensed Warrick.

The house was littered with red plastic cups, empty alcohol bottles, and trays of food. The scent of pizza mingled with the scent of alcohol and blended with the pounding music in an energy that spoke to my incubus nature of a very good place to hunt for food. The darker side of my nature said it would be an excellent way to find prey. An incubus who drained a human dry wouldn't have to feed for months. Some went so far as to develop a harem of slaves to feed from. Fortunately, I'd never been that way and certainly wasn't now. That had cost me power in the past, but it had certainly worked out in my favor.

Mal and I found our way into the living room where a bunch of expectant women had put Warrick, waiting for a show.

He was currently keeping them happy with a subtle application of power while he stalled for time, probably anticipating a rescue.

The other incubus's eyes lit up when he saw Mal and me.

"Thank you," he mouthed.

"You sure about this, Mal?" I murmured as we threaded our way through the drunk crowd.

"Yeah, just give them a show, don't let them get too touchy feely, and stock up on energy. I have a feeling Chris and I are going to have to deal with this vampire problem, and she's going to need you to help watch the pizza shop. I wouldn't mind if you helped at the store. Chris won't mind."

Mal was right. The only time she expected me to deny my nature was when I was around her employees, and that was completely reasonable. I was still a little nervous about this, but I knew Chris wouldn't be upset. She had agreed to me going after Warrick, after all. And truthfully, I didn't even have to do much. A careful application of my powers would provide most of what the drunk women really wanted, anyway. Well, drunk people, there were a few men in the crowd.

"Ladies and gentlefolk," Mal said, his intoxicating voice laced with a touch of his own vampiric powers. "You have mistakenly abducted the pizza man."

Warrick waved sheepishly.

"What!" someone shouted. A few others added dismayed comments.

"Hot pizza guy!" another called.

"Never fear. Sabian here"—he pointed at me—"is the real entertainment."

I bowed while Mal hooked his arm with Warrick's and guided him away. I replaced his thread of power with my own, and soon all eyes were on me.

The music shifted to something I could easily dance to. I swung my hips and strutted around the makeshift stage they'd set up for the party, making lingering eye contact with a handful of the women. The energy flowed into me far faster than it was flowing out and... I didn't like it.

It was filling and had good energy, but it wasn't from Chris or any of our household. It felt wrong.

Still, I wanted to make sure the party was happy since we were taking their "stripper" away. Maybe it was me being nice. Maybe I was torturing myself a little. I'd give them just enough of a show that I could easily fill in the rest with my incubus powers and then get out of here. I wasn't even upset that I no longer liked feeding from anyone else. I'd take the energy, and I'd know for the future that I was well and truly Chris's demon in all ways.

Keeping a sultry smile plastered on my face, I hooked my fingers under my t-shirt, much to the delight of the crowd. They cheered. I teased them, lifting it, and then dancing away again. Finally, I pulled my shirt over my head and let them get an eyeful of my abs.

While they fixed that image in their minds, I carefully crafted the rest of the routine, sending out the energy that would let them remember a fabulous strip tease, not quite remember my face, and blame any lacks on the alcohol. They more than made up for the increased energy demands with their lust and enjoyment.

I certainly didn't feel bad about slipping out when I did. They were happy, and even though I hadn't enjoyed myself the way I would have before Chris, I was well fed and would be able to easily survive if Chris and Mal were gone for a while. Besides, Aaron would still be around. I suspected Chris would need Brennan, too. If I got desperate, Aaron would do me a solid, I was sure. And if not, Ezra could supply me with energy directly. Normally a prince would never stoop to helping a mere minion level demon like that, but our relationship was different thanks to Chris.

As soon as I was clear of the sated partiers, I pulled my shirt back on and hurried out of the house.

The others were waiting for me. Though I was surprised Warrick and Mandy hadn't left yet.

The other incubus gave me a sheepish look. "I wasn't sure what to do. Thanks for the save."

I laughed. "You did the right thing. Using your powers to keep them happy while waiting for rescue kept them from any negative associations with the pizza parlor—and kept you safe from drunk women."

Mandy was tucked under his arm, and I sensed no annoyance from her toward Warrick, just gratitude that everything had turned out okay.

"I pulled off my shirt, danced around a little, and fed them a story with my powers that should keep them satisfied." I didn't share how distasteful it had been. I didn't want Warrick to hesitate to call for a rescue in the future.

"All right, it's been a long-ass day. Let's get out of here." Mal gestured toward the vehicles.

Mandy sighed. "We gotta head back to the shop and at least finish up for the night. Billy knows we were delayed. He was professional over the phone, but he's going to laugh his ass off."

"Well, you do have an incubus riding around with you," I pointed out with a grin. "Don't worry, when you work for Price's, you have to be understanding about weird shit."

Mandy laughed. "Truth. Okay. Thanks, guys. I really appreciate the save." She hugged Mal and me and gave Brennan a wave before dragging Warrick back to the pizza shop's car.

I shook my head and got into the back seat of Mal's car while Brennan folded himself into the front. Mal was shorter than either of us, and his choice of car reflected his lack of height.

"Are you okay, Sabian?" Mal glanced at me in the rearview mirror once he was on the road.

"Yes. But I certainly don't want to do that again if I don't have to. The days of me wanting to feed from energy not generated by us are long past."

Mal raised his eyebrows. "Interesting."

"Yeah, surprised me, too. I'm all stocked up, and I do get a bit of a trickle from Chris, like right now with Ezra at the house. So, I'll be fine if you are gone for a while."

"Hopefully dealing with this problem won't take much time or things could really get out of hand."

"You should take Brennan, too."

"I was going to suggest that," Brennan said. "Ideally, Lucifer or Ezra would join us, but I suspect they'll be tied up in Hell."

"Hopefully not literally," Mal replied, stopping briefly at a stop sign.

I laughed, not quite quick enough to banish a thought of Ezra wrapped up in Mal's ropes. Chris would love it. I doubted Ezra would allow it, however.

"Do we need to drive around for a while?" Brennan glanced back at me.

"Uh, no, I think normal house rules are sufficient." Normal house rules being that Chris usually confined sex to one of the bedrooms and the rest of us were free to move about as we would. Not that Mal, Aaron, or I would have raised an eyebrow at just about anything, but Brennan, Ezra, and Lucifer were more private, and we all did our best to respect that. If any of us wanted to use the rest of the house for sex, we just let the others know. I wasn't sure if Chris was aware we had a system, but so far it had worked out well for everyone.

"Good. Let's go home, then." Brennan leaned back in the seat and gazed out the window.

It made me glad to hear and feel how much he meant that. He truly felt at home with Chris and the rest of us now, and considering his background, that was huge.

All in all, it had been an educational evening. I just hoped whatever this vampire thing was, Mal and Chris and Brennan could solve it quickly. Not to mention these other hunters and the run-in Chris had in Thailand a few weeks ago. I was looking forward to things being quiet for a while.

CHAPTER 10

Ezra

"**I** have a message to pass along," I murmured as I helped Chris slide off her black leather coat.

"Can it wait?"

I kissed the curve of her neck where it met her shoulder, the faint taste of garlic clinging to her from her pizza parlor. I wasn't even sure if she'd been there, but the jacket held the scent, too.

"If I wait, I'll forget. It's important, but not earth shattering." I nipped her gently, knowing she liked it, and was rewarded with a pleased groan. She pressed her back into my chest, and I almost missed the hook when I tried to hang her jacket.

"Okay, fine. What's up?" She leaned more of her weight against my chest and gave a contented sigh.

I trailed my fingers up her stomach, skin tingling as I felt the various wards and marks we'd placed on her. I never would have thought I'd have fallen so completely for a human, but fallen I had. I blessed the day I'd been forced to possess her to save her life, and everything that had come since.

Her hellhound, who had chosen to appear like a fluffy Pomeranian for his earthly form, wagged his tail when I glanced at him. He was part of my breeding program and had been a gift to Chris long before I'd realized what she'd come to mean to me.

"It seems that the demons are extremely fond of you. So fond, in fact, that they want to challenge you. Some are even training."

She stepped away and turned to face me, the loss of body contact almost painful after a week away.

"Say what now?"

"The demons want to duel with you and they're training."

Chris shut her eyes, her shoulders rising and falling with a deep sigh before she spoke. "Should I be worried?"

"No. Just be prepared to duel next time you're wandering around Hell."

"You say that like it's no big deal." A brief flash of concern crossed her face.

I chuckled. "I'm fairly certain you could take on Lucifer. I wouldn't worry about the others."

"You say *that* like it's no big deal, too, and I'm not reassured." She poked me in the chest.

I grabbed her finger and brought her hand to my lips, kissing her knuckles. "It'll be fine. If you want to avoid the duels, then just avoid going anywhere but my fortress or Lucifer's."

"Right. Easy as that." She shook her head. "Well, I'm guessing I only have you for the night, so let's not worry about the other demons."

"Would you like me to seduce you first?"

"Nope. Let's get straight to the sex." She grinned and pulled me back to the main bedroom.

I had zero problem with that, though I made a note to find some time to take her out properly soon.

"How are things here?" I followed, enjoying the possessive tug on my hand as she hurried me along.

"Peachy. Shop's in good shape. Flame demons showing up in the kitchen to buy pizza. Bachelorette party trying to turn one of my people into a stripper. Some genius made a carpet-shaped summoning board and ran a robot vacuum over it. Summoned a few demons and a really obnoxious ghost. Normal stuff."

"I can't tell if you're joking or not." I opened the door to her bedroom and followed my exorcist inside.

She laughed. "I'm not joking."

"If we have time later, you have to fill me in."

Chris turned after the door was shut and pushed me gently against the wall. She ran her hands down my chest. The feel of her fingers sliding over my skin with just my silky dress shirt between us was exquisite.

I cupped her cheek and leaned forward for a kiss. She obliged, hungrily melding her lips to mine as she molded her body against me. With the press of her breasts against my chest, and the feel of her hands as they stroked my sides, I was more than ready to magic her clothing away and drag her to the bed.

Still, I let Chris set the pace. After exploring my body for a while, she slowly, almost sensually, flicked the buttons of my shirt open. Starting at the top, she worked her way down the shirt, being sure to drag her fingers across my chest in between buttons.

I let her work, enjoying the sensations of being touched and undressed by the woman I loved. Once she had the shirt open, her fingers explored my chest, dragging through my chest hair and over the muscles until she found the mark she'd placed on me months earlier. My entire being tingled when she dragged her fingers over the visible lines of the pizza pentagram.

Her eyes shuttered as she enjoyed the feeling through the connection our shared mark gave us.

I let her play, but once she finished, I shrugged out of the shirt and tugged her t-shirt off over her head. Her bra went next, and I cupped her breasts, pebbling her nipples with my thumbs while her breathing quickened, and her eyes shone with lust.

Chris enjoyed foreplay, but what she really wanted was sex and then cuddles after, and it didn't take long before she was unbuttoning and unzipping my pants so they could slide off my hips. She didn't give me time to get her out of her jeans, just kicked them off and yanked the comforter back off the bed.

"I would very much like you more than once tonight," she said.

That she was so direct, so forceful in her desires, was the hottest damn thing and one of the many reasons I loved her.

"How would you like me to take you?"

"Mmmm, dealer's choice." She then flipped over on her stomach and stuck her rear in the air, letting me know she was the dealer in this case.

"Always a good choice," I said, kneeling behind her.

I spread her legs wider and shifted her position slightly until I could get my mouth on her.

She moaned appreciatively and pushed against my face, encouraging me. I knew her body well, the way she liked to be stroked, licked, nibbled, and just when to enter her with my fingers and just how to curl my fingers to get her screaming my name.

And hearing her shout in ecstasy had me rock hard and weeping and barely able to contain myself as I stared at her beautiful ass and her dripping wet pussy. She wiggled her butt as if to say, "less looking, more pounding," or maybe I was hearing her thoughts through our bond.

Either way, it was time to slide myself inside her, relish her heat as it closed around my cock and make sure she got at least one more orgasm before I had my own release.

I dug my fingers into her hips with just the right amount of pressure for her to enjoy and slid myself in and out of her a few times to make sure she was ready for a pounding.

The feeling of her warmth, tight and slick around me, was akin to what I imagined Heaven might be like. Pure bliss. The needy gasps and moans sent tingles through my entire body, and her urgent cries letting me know she was close to coming again almost brought me over the edge. But no. Chris first. Besides, this felt so good, I had no desire to end things that quickly.

She panted before shouting, her inner walls tightening down on my cock in waves and destroying my resolve that I would try to last longer.

Pleasure surged through me as I spilled into her. I clutched at her hips, shuddering with my own orgasm and reveling in the sensations we were able to share through our mark. It was almost like getting two orgasms at the same time, nearly overwhelming, and it took me a bit of time before I was able to withdraw and hold Chris against my chest.

"Ezra, my prince." She kissed my neck. "I do hope you're up for more after a bit. That was exceptional, especially for a quickie."

I laughed. "I agree and yes, we've got all night. I'll keep you up for at least half of it."

She tilted her head so she could meet my gaze. "Good. I'll hold you to that."

She would, too. Though I'd worked myself into a position as a prince so I'd only ever have to bend knee to one being ever again, I'd fallen hard for this exorcist and I'd get on my knees for her, any time.

CHAPTER 11

Aaron

My feet dragged and my shoulders slumped with exhaustion like I'd rarely felt since grad school. If I didn't absolutely know the cause of why I was so tired, I'd suspect supernatural interference. This project at work and the long hours it required were kicking my ass. I'd missed dinner. Again. And I'd almost slept at the office, but I'd done that too many times recently. I'd even missed a visit from Ezra yesterday. Though I imagined Chris had kept him occupied.

The house was nearly empty when I pushed open the door. I couldn't hear or sense any of the normal occupants. The demons always pinged on my senses as potential enemies, despite knowing they were friends. The same with Mal. Part of being Nephilim. Brennan was different. He just felt "other" for lack of a better term. I did sense Mayhem and Chris. Chris hit all sorts of interesting feelings when I studied her with my supernatural abilities. Lust tinged all the colors of her aura, my lust for her, that was. She felt a touch demonic, a touch dangerous—okay a lot dangerous—a touch human, and a fair bit of that same "other" that Brennan had. My sense of her had evolved as her abilities and ties to the demons had evolved.

I was glad Chris was home, and while I wouldn't have minded the others around, the day had been hard, and a quiet house wouldn't break my heart. I rubbed my temples and kicked off my shoes, not really paying attention to my surroundings, so it took me a minute to notice Chris leaning against the wall, her arms crossed under her breasts and a small smirk on her very kissable lips.

"Chris!" I winced. I even sounded surprised.

Her smirk broadened into a wide smile. "Aaron, how are you?"

"Fuck." I breathed out in response, shoulders sagging even more.

She chuckled. "Work that bad right now?"

"It's just really intense."

She didn't ask, knowing it was classified. "Are you going in tomorrow?"

I shook my head, relieved to be able to say no. "We are at a point where we all decided we needed at least a weekend, or we were going to start making mistakes. The work is time sensitive, but it's critical to get it right."

"Good." She pushed off the wall and sauntered toward me. "This is a seduction."

"A what now?"

She grabbed my hand, and something else caught my eye that should have been obvious right off, but my exhausted brain hadn't kept up with what my eyes were seeing. Chris wore one of my shirts. It was practically a dress on her.

That was it. A dark green shirt. Nothing else.

"Mal made dinner for us." She guided me to a chair.

I sat, and she poured a glass of red wine and set it in front of me.

"I can help." I tried to get back up, and she put a hand on my shoulder.

"My love, let me take care of you tonight."

Her voice was a soft purr that went straight to my center and almost got my exhausted body to respond. A little food and I might even be up for more after a bit.

She dimmed the lights and lit a handful of candles she'd placed on the table. The light played across her skin, accenting the shadows, and making me jealous that it was touching her and I wasn't. I watched as she went back into the kitchen, her ass shifting enticingly under my shirt and her bare legs just begging for attention. Yes, I was definitely going to be up for more after dinner.

Whatever Mal had made for us smelled delightful, and yet I was willing to skip it for a chance to feast on Chris, but I hadn't eaten all day and especially for someone with my metabolism, that wasn't the best. I needed to take a minute for some fuel.

She returned carrying two plates, one piled high for me and a slightly more modest amount for herself. It was some sort of chicken over pasta in a cream sauce. Lemon twists on the side garnished it. She set the plates on the table then kissed my cheek before scooting into her own chair. I swear she wiggled in the chair just enough to reveal almost everything but still hide the extra interesting bits. The tattoos and wards that covered her body seemed alive on her skin in the flickering candlelight, and I wanted to explore them with my tongue.

"Aaron, you must keep your strength up. Eat." She gestured at me with her fork before stuffing a bite in her mouth then slowly drawing the fork out.

I groaned.

"Eat."

"As you command." As soon as I put some of the food in my mouth I was groaning for a different reason. "Mal's outdone himself."

Chris murmured her agreement.

We made short work of the food, and I declined seconds, though I could have eaten more. I wanted dessert.

When Chris returned after clearing the table, I swore she'd undone all but a few strategic buttons.

Her coy smile brought me the rest of the way to full hardness.

"I would like dessert, my dear exorcist." I reached for her.

"How would you like it?" She came to my side, one hand resting lightly on my shoulder.

"Most people eat at the table." I licked my lips in anticipation.

She grinned at me. I shifted around and gripped her hips. She put her hands on my shoulders, and I lifted until her butt was on the table. I ran a hand gently down her leg, over her calf muscles and picked up her foot, giving it a quick massage before putting it on the arm of the chair and repeating the process with her other.

"Lay back, let me feast upon you."

She complied, spreading her knees and moaning softly when I ran my fingers gently up her thighs before finding the handful of buttons she'd left fastened. Once they were open, I stared at her laying on the table, my shirt spread beneath her, breasts, stomach, pussy, and everything bared to me. The candlelight played over her body, and I wanted to join it.

Her sigh of pleasure as my lips closed on her pussy, my tongue exploring her folds, made me even harder. I didn't take my time, instead going straight to her favorite spots with one hand on her breast, sliding a finger inside her with the other, and my lips on her clit.

Before long, she was crying my name, back arching up off the table as an orgasm wracked her. Damn, we should recreate the scene with one of the guys so I could watch. My current view looking up her body from her pussy was divine. I suspected the view of her splayed out on the table was positively sinful.

"Your turn?" she finally managed.

"Ride me." I trailed kisses up her stomach. "Realistically, you might only get me to come once, and I'd like to be inside you when I do."

"Totally fair," she stroked my arm, raising goosebumps on my flesh.

I pushed the chair back and cast about for a good spot. This chair had arms, but the one next to me did not. She nodded her agreement and pulled her foot back so I could switch chairs.

She made sliding off the table seductive, and I might have drooled a little as she sauntered over to me, my shirt hanging from her shoulders, her arms still in the sleeves, but the rest open. Chris straddled my thighs, ran her hands down my chest, and settled at the button to my fly.

"Mmmm, looks like someone is ready after all."

"You always know how to turn me on." I wasn't very good at pillow talk, but she'd once told me I could talk physics at her—her phrasing—and she'd find it sexy.

As soon as Chris had me free, she moved until she was positioned over me. I took my cock in one hand and helped guide it as she lowered slowly, impaling herself. The way her eyes fluttered shut as I stretched her just made my own pleasure more intense as she took me inside herself, her wet warmth caging me.

"Mmmm, so good. I love the way you feel inside me, Aaron."

"Your pleasure is my pleasure." I gripped her hips with my hands.

When she was ready, I thrust into her and she rode me, eyes shut, mouth parted, gasps of pleasure turning into intense cries of need, of desire, of a feeling so extreme she couldn't keep it controlled.

When her inner walls rippled around my cock, it was enough to bring me over the edge with my own shout echoing her cries. Her body trembled and she rested her head on my shoulder while we held each other, still joined, both with our bodies, and the mystical mark we shared.

"Aaron, I love you."

"I love you, Chris."

I could feel her lips curve into a smile against my neck where she rested her head. Yes, I regretted nothing about the events that had brought us together, and her seduction tonight touched me deeply.

"So, after you get some rest, I want you again in the morning." She nipped my neck playfully. "And maybe some more throughout the day. Need to take advantage of your weekend off."

"Oh, hell yes," I breathed, and lifted her, cock going hard inside her again. Maybe I would get off more than once tonight, after all.

She squirmed happily as I carried her toward the main bedroom, still riding my cock, her legs wrapped around my waist, and her arms around my shoulders. Her tiny motions sent thrills jolting through me until I couldn't take it anymore and shoved her up against the nearest wall.

Her delighted laugh just urged me on, until she was crying out again. Maybe I could pull a few more orgasms out of her before we made it to the bedroom. The challenge delighted me, and I looked for the next spot while she clung to me.

Yes, this was shaping out to be just the weekend I needed. It had been too long since my exorcist had been in my arms. Far too long.

CHAPTER 12

Price

For a while, I let the smell of marinara, the chatter of my employees, and the practiced motion of spinning pizza dough occupy my mind. I'd spent the last few days ignoring the rest of the world and catching up with Ezra and Aaron, but I couldn't ignore the problems anymore. I hadn't seen any more activity from the group that had attacked me and Lucifer, but now there was another hunter group around and they seemed quite competent, even though I'd laughed at them. I'd been laughing at the absurdity of their accusations, not their abilities. Still, it had been a couple of weeks, and I hadn't seen anything from the hunters, either. Nor had anything weird popped up on our radar in regards to the vampiric creature they were after. Mal had quietly started looking into it, and so far, nothing. I hadn't talked with Lucifer about it, and I probably needed to, but I was strangely worried about going back to Hell after Ezra's warning.

I spun the last crust onto a pizza board and handed it off to Rebecca so she could finish putting it together and get it in the oven. A quick glance around the kitchen let me know all was in order. The dining area was full on this Saturday night, and by the sound of it, everything ran smoothly and if we had any supernatural guests, they were in disguise. Or they simply hadn't caused a stir.

Grateful the pizza shop was operating normally, I headed back to my office. Billy was at the computer working on all the paperwork I'd assigned him since I was here to help on the floor.

"Going okay?"

"Yeah, Boss. Thanks." He squinted at the screen.

"Need glasses?"

Billy grunted. "No, just tired. Haven't been sleeping well."

"Anything wrong?" I hoped not.

"No."

"Why don't you take the rest of the night off? This will all keep." I didn't want any of my employees to work themselves so much they were stressed about coming here. Of course, if they were stressed about the demons, that was different. I didn't want that, either.

Billy sighed and pushed back from the computer. "It's not that. I'd rather be here. It's just quiet at home." He rubbed his forehead. "I lost my kitty a few days ago, and it's just not the same without her. She was old."

Mayhem, my constant shadow, woofed softly and hopped up into Billy's lap.

"Oh, I'm sorry, mate. That's tough. If you'd rather be here, that's fine. But if you need a couple of days, just tell me. Okay?"

He nodded, wiping away a tear and glancing at me for a moment before refocusing on the computer.

I could tell he wanted me to leave, so I stepped out, wondering if there was anything I could do to help. It didn't escape my notice that Mayhem stayed behind to comfort Billy.

The problem distracted me from the rest of my concerns for a bit as I headed out to wander the dining area and check in with the customers. Maybe there was a feline equivalent to a hellhound? Maybe Billy would like a demon cat? I wasn't even sure if that was a good idea or not. I'd run it past Ezra.

Aaron came in just as I was finishing my rounds, looking drained, even with his weekend off. Speaking of someone who was working too hard…

"Hey." I gave him a hug and pulled him over to the bar.

"Hey," he replied, his normally deep, resonant voice flat with exhaustion. Aaron rested his elbows on the bar top and leaned his head against his hands.

I got him his favorite beer and some pizza knots that someone had made and not served.

Aaron took a deep breath and sat up to take a drink.

"Thanks, love." He gave me a tired smile.

"You're working too hard." I had no idea what his project was. It truthfully didn't matter to me other than that I had no way of helping him other than to be understanding. Classified work and all that. Our time together helped him forget for a while, but his work never waited on the sidelines for long.

"We're almost done." He slowly chewed a pizza knot.

"Okay."

Just then the door banged open. I looked up to Asher and Perl entering, faces tense.

Damn it. It was as if thinking of them had summoned them into my restaurant. Asher's dark eyes were narrowed in anger. The expression didn't deepen when he saw me watching him. Maybe the little shit's anger wasn't directed at me.

Perl's expression was blank, as if she'd seen things she'd rather not. That set off an entirely different set of alarm bells.

Mandy wasn't in tonight, so Stacy had hostess duties. After a quick discussion, she brought them over to a couple of open places at the bar.

"What can I get you to drink?" I asked since I was here.

"Water," Asher grumbled.

Perl nodded.

"Want anything to eat?"

"Sure." He ran his hand through his dark curls.

I traded a glance with Aaron before throwing in a basic pizza order for them.

"So, what's up?" I leaned against the bar when I came back.

"We need your help." Perl put her hands on the bar and stared at me, ignoring Asher's glare, now turned on her.

"My help?"

"Becca and Gael tangled with some humans who claimed to be working for God. We were just arriving to help when literal demons showed up and yanked them all through a portal." Perl's voice was a little higher pitched than normal.

"Well, that's something." It was my turn to bury my face in my hands.

"Can you help us? You're an exorcist." Asher fixed his glare on me. "We need our friends back. They've done nothing to deserve whatever torment they are currently undergoing."

I shared a glanced with Aaron before shaking my head in resignation. Guess I wasn't going to avoid Hell after all.

"All right, let's head back to my place." Reluctantly, I stood and the hunters followed.

***

"No, you're not going with me!" I couldn't even believe we were having this discussion. Why would they want to go to Hell? I didn't even want to go.

Asher and Perl looked between me and the portal on a wall in my basement, determined sets to both of their expressions.

"We're going!"

"It's Hell!"

"*You're* going," Asher gestured angrily toward the portal.

"I'm not excited about it, but at least I'll be relatively safe."

"How?" Perl shoved her fists onto her hips.

"How what?"

"How are you safe?" She clarified.

"I'm not. I can just fight back. That makes me safer."

"We can fight," Asher insisted.

"Not a bunch of demons, on their own turf, in Hell." They couldn't get through the portal without me, so I wasn't worried about them following, but I didn't want them trying and fucking things up either.

"Why do you have a portal to Hell in your basement," Asher finally said into the silence our stare down had created.

"Mate, I thought that'd be your first question." I shook my head.

"Well?" Perl encouraged.

Shrugging, I gave them the answer I'd come up with on the ride over. It wasn't a lie; it just wasn't the whole truth. "When we were averting the apocalypse, I had to get back and forth a few times. I'm on good terms with one of the princes, and the portal goes to his fortress. It's a relatively safe entrance to Hell." I wrinkled my nose. I needed to stop using the words safe and Hell in the same sentence.

"You are a very interesting woman, Chris Price," Asher finally said.

"Yeah. Well. You're still not coming with me. I don't want to have to protect you while I'm watching my back."

Sabian finally joined us, along with Mayhem. I'd asked him to accompany me, since he actually *was* a demon, and of course my hellhound was coming along. If nothing else, he'd want to romp with his relatives. Aaron, Mal, and Brennan were upstairs avoiding the hunters.

"So, why are you bringing pretty boy? He's big, but he doesn't look like a fighter." Perl put her hands on her hips.

Sabian gave a slight bow. "I'm a lover, not a fighter," he agreed amicably, before wandering over to the portal and pushing through.

At a guess, he didn't want to mess with the hunters, either. After a moment, he leaned back out, grinning at me. "All clear, Chris." He vanished again.

Before I could warn her, Perl darted at the wall. She smacked into the portal like she'd hit a concrete wall, screeching in pain and frustration, blood pouring from her nose.

"It's keyed," I said. "Now, please stay here. I'll see if I can find out what happened to them. If I can get them back quickly, I will. If not, I'll return and let you know what my plan is."

Asher put his arms around Perl and helped her into a chair.

"How long should we wait?" Resignation flattened his voice.

"A couple of hours. The guys know you're down here. Try not to cause too many problems."

Perl managed to look offended around her bloody nose.

I turned away from the hunters and just as I was about to step into the portal, someone slammed into my back.

In the moments before my wards triggered, we were through the portal, and then a wave of energy slammed the person off me and threw them backward. I was honestly surprised they'd even managed to get that close, though intent made a huge difference.

I spun and saw Perl sprawled in the red dust, curling around herself and gasping in the unnatural chill of one of Hell's many barren plains.

"And why the fuck are we on the plains?" I belatedly threw up a defensive shield and hurried to her side.

We were alone. Not in the location the portal was supposed to let us out in, and likely soon to be surrounded by demons. How had we ended up here? And where were Sabian and Mayhem?

Fuck.

Dakota Brown

CHAPTER 13

Mandy

I slammed the door on my car and sank back into the seat, waiting a moment before turning the ignition. It wasn't a million degrees in the car, so I let the lingering warmth from the day soak into my sore muscles. It hadn't been a bad day, just a long one. There were rarely any truly bad days at the pizza shop, but it was now my weekend, and I was excited for some uninterrupted quality time with Warrick. We were going hiking tomorrow, but tonight... tonight we had other plans.

He said he had a surprise for me and had stayed home since I didn't have a delivery shift at work.

Wondering what the incubus could possibly have done for me had kept me occupied all day at work. Now that I'd had a moment of Zen time, I turned on my car and headed for home. It took some work not to speed all the way back to my apartment, but getting pulled over wouldn't get me home faster.

I marveled at how much life had changed in the last few months. The thing with the apocalypse, and finding out that the supernatural really did exist, and Mal... I really loved that man. Not like wanting to steal him away from Chris love. Not at all. One, I knew it wasn't possible. Two, it was more of an extreme affection for an older brother tinted by the tiniest bit of a crush. I would be lying if I didn't admit that I'd had a huge crush on him before, but nothing I would ever have tried to act on. Now that I had Warrick, well, my needs were more than fulfilled, and I loved my incubus. So, it was more of a tiny crush and a lot of love. Mal had saved my life, and he was always there to help when I needed it. I couldn't forget how he and Chris had gone out with me several times after I'd been abducted so that I could enjoy a night out without having to worry about my safety. Chris was more than my boss, she was family.

That musing kept me distracted long enough to get home without breaking speed records. I lived in a relatively cheap area in a strip of apartments. It wasn't too bad, and I liked it well enough, but someday I wanted a house.

I parked in my spot and headed for my door, semi alert for trouble. I'd never seen anything happen here, but that didn't mean I wanted to get kidnapped again. Our doors had keypads in addition to locks. I keyed my code and went inside.

The scent of something floral warred with the garlic that permeated my skin and clothes. I kicked off my shoes and noticed a rose on the floor.

Not trying to stifle my grin, I dropped my keys and purse onto the table, bent to pick up the rose, and saw another. He'd left me a trail of colorful roses. This first was white. The next, yellow. The third, red. He'd even found purple and one that had been dyed in a rainbow theme. When I moved through the living room, following and collecting the trail of flowers, I found a bouquet of wildflowers and another dozen red roses. The wildflowers were of a more mountain variety than what we had in Santa Fe, and I wondered where he had gotten them. They were beautiful, with forget-me-nots, snap dragons, paintbrush flowers, and others along with some beautiful long grasses.

I put the roses I'd collected into an empty vase set on a table for the purpose. The flowers distracted me from the other marvel in my living room. Warrick had laid out a large rug that, judging from the portable clawfoot bathtub he'd set on it, was probably at least water resistant to protect the floor. It was strewn with flower petals. The tub, which I certainly hadn't owned before and honestly wasn't sure how he'd gotten in the front door, let alone filled, was the kind that you could fully submerge in. Hell, both of us could probably submerge in it.

He must have used some sort of demonic power.

I just stared.

"Like it?" Warrick's low, rumbling voice caressed me. He was a little shorter than Sabian, with darker, dusky skin. My incubus was lean, strong and had delicious dark chocolate hair and rich brown eyes. The depths of the ocean seemed to peer out at me from those deep brown eyes. Terrifying, yet comforting and intriguing at the same time.

"It's amazing," I breathed.

He came around behind me, hands going to my shoulders and kneading away the tension. I sighed and let him work on my shoulders for a minute or three.

"Let's get you undressed and in the bath."

"I'm all garlicy." I felt a little dumb protesting about being dirty before getting into a bath, but it was so nice, and I was sure he was going to join me.

"Take a quick shower first if you want."

I laughed as he took my hand and led us into the bedroom. "Cleaning up to take a bath seems silly."

"However you'll be most comfortable, sunshine."

"Mmm, I like that. Sunshine, huh?"

The incubus pressed his lips to my neck. "Yeah. You're my sunshine."

Not able to stop grinning at the silly pet name, I let him undress me and pull me into the bathroom.

His gaze roamed my body, a grin playing at his lips. I wasn't the height of beauty or fashion, but I thought I looked all right. Warrick certainly thought so, too. I didn't even mind that it was at least partially his incubus nature that let him appreciate my soft curves, the slight chub at my waist, and my small breasts. He said they were perfect. I was just happy he liked them. I'd never been too body conscious, but it was nice to be appreciated.

"Shower fast, sunshine."

"Yes—" I hesitated. He'd given me a pet name. Maybe I should have one for him. His eyes reminded me of the ocean depths but the first thing that came to my mind, squid, wasn't really the best pet name.

Warrick tilted his head as he caught the stray thought. "Squid?"

"Uh—Cuddle fish?"

He burst out laughing. "Try them out until you find one you like, sunshine."

Getting used to living with a mildly telepathic being had been interesting. Chris had actually spent a little time with me after Lucifer had dropped Warrick in my lap. She'd told me some things to expect when dealing with demons, and that had been one. At first I'd felt self-conscious about it. Warrick had promised not to do it on purpose. Though he had made sure I knew that by his very nature he couldn't turn the ability completely off.

"Okay, clown fish."

Warrick chuckled. "Shower. I'm anxious to try out the bath."

"How did you get it in here, anyway?"

Warrick winked and turned the water on for me.

Taking the hint, I climbed in and scrubbed off the sweat and garlic. I used a strong-smelling soap that was the only one I'd found that seemed to negate the pizza smell without being revolting.

When I exited, Warrick wrapped me in a large, fluffy towel I didn't remember owning. It was somehow warmed to the perfect temperature. More magic? I curled up into his arms.

"You truly think that?" His breath tickled my ear as he spoke.

I sensed some insecurity from Warrick and snuggled closer. "Yes, my dearest angler fish. I am the luckiest girl alive to have you."

The ridiculous pet name, along with the sincerity in my voice, eased the tension I'd momentarily felt from him.

"Should I get you an encyclopedia of the ocean?"

I laughed. "The internet will probably do."

"You want me to get you the internet? All of it? I am but one demon. That's a mighty task."

Giggling, I shoved him playfully. He didn't budge. Instead, he gathered me up in his arms in a bridal carry and took me out into the living room, setting me down on the rug. He tugged my towel away and offered me a hand so I could climb into the tub.

Despite having been there for a while, the water was the perfect temperature. I wiggled my toes in pleasure and rapidly sank down into the lightly scented water.

"Is it all right if I join you?"

"I was hoping you would."

Warrick shed his clothing, and I was momentarily distracted from my physical pleasure by the eye candy he presented. Everything about Warrick was a perfect complement to me. His height, just right for me to tuck under his arm and feel safe. His physique? Somehow, he'd figured out my ideal body type when I hadn't even known it. The size of his, uh, other parts, exactly the right dimensions for my maximum pleasure.

I'd have almost felt bad, since I knew incubi were basically shape shifters and he'd chosen this form specifically to please me, but Chris had assured me that the sex demons got just as much out of pleasing their partners, if not more, as their partners did.

Warrick slid gracefully into the tub of lightly scented water and reclined across from me. He leaned forward and slid one strong hand down my calf before cupping my heel and drawing my foot toward him.

He applied his fingers to working the knots out of my foot muscles.

"Oh my gods," I murmured.

"Good?"

"I've never had a foot massage before. This is amazing."

"Just wait until I get to your hands." His low voice was full of promise.

"That sounds even better."

I let myself melt while he worked on my body, moving from my feet to my calves, and upward until he was gently rubbing my temples and running his hands through my wet hair. I'd never felt this relaxed in my life.

"Now, you can choose. Would you like another type of massage, or would you like me to dry you off and take you to bed for the night?"

I had been hovering on the edge of sleep, but I did not want to miss out on this other type of massage. I'd gone too long without having a regular partner. No way was I too tired for sex tonight.

"I want all the massages." I opened my eyes in time to see a delighted grin curling Warrick's lips.

"I'm so glad." He went to work on my body, this time tracing his fingers down my front, cupping my breasts, knowing they were extremely sensitive.

I arched up into his touch. "Warrick, that feels so damn good." He continued to stroke with one hand, leaning over, taking one of my nipples in his mouth, and sucking.

"Oh fuck." I arched again, body shuddering as he brought me to an orgasm with his lips and masterful touch.

Warrick rumbled happily and worked his hands lower down my stomach, gently massaging as he went. When he cupped my hips, digging his fingers in tightly, I lifted and he slid his knees under me, pulling me close and pressing my chest to his. His erection rubbed between my legs, massaging me there while he kneaded my butt with his fingers.

I slid against him, using his body to bring pleasure to myself.

He twitched against me, rumbling again with the pleasure he got both from the physical contact and the lustful energy I sent his way.

"Fuck, Mandy," he growled. "You're the best thing that's ever happened to me."

"You too, electric eel."

He snorted, nibbling at my neck before sliding one hand between my legs and caressing my folds.

"You're already so wet," he breathed into my ear.

"I'm in the water."

"And you're being naughty, my sunshine. Do you need a spanking?" He nipped a touch harder, and denied me his fingers, pulling them away. Especially since I'd recently been abducted, he'd been very gentle with me, but every now and again he pushed my comfort zone slightly. Never more than I could handle.

"Maybe I just need you to fill me, so I have something else to think about besides being naughty."

The water level suddenly dropped—definitely demon magic—leaving his cock above the water.

"Fill your mouth with this, then," he ordered.

I could refuse and he'd be okay with it, so I didn't have a problem with him telling me what to do. It was a game he'd never abuse so I moved backward off his legs and bent over, taking his cock in my mouth. The salty taste of pre-cum mingled with the water.

I sucked, then hummed as I worked my lips on his velvety length.

Warrick shuddered, murmuring in appreciation, hands tightening on my body as he grew harder in my mouth.

"Now, I think I should fill other parts of you," he said after a short time. "Otherwise, you'll get more than you prefer."

I gave him one last suck before letting his cock slide out of my mouth.

He wiped away a bit of drool I'd worked up then leaned me back against the tub and once again stroked my folds. This time he didn't comment on how moist I was, just slid his fingers inside me and stroked. I bucked my hips, thrusting against his fingers, panting as my body tightened, so ready for another release. He brought me to the brink of another orgasm before pulling his fingers out.

I cried out in frustration.

"Patience, my sunshine."

"Mudfish," I muttered in annoyance.

"I don't think mudfish live in the ocean. Perhaps I should go look that up real quick."

"Hey!" I grabbed his arm and pulled him back toward me, knowing he was playing, but unable to help myself.

Warrick laughed. He was still on his knees as he grabbed my hips and lifted. I put my hands on his shoulders for balance and spread my legs so he could slide me down onto his cock.

My soft cries became loud ones as he thrust into me, his hard length bringing me back to the edge of orgasm. This time, blessedly, he didn't stop, possibly even adding a touch of his powers to send me spiraling over the edge into near oblivion as my body clamped down on his, ripples of intense pleasure thrumming through me all the way to my fingers and toes.

I slumped in his arms, and he held me, still hard inside me—incubus powers were immensely useful—and I relaxed, enjoying being held. Somehow the water level had risen again, and it cradled both of us.

"I love you, Warrick," I murmured.

"I love you, Mandy. More?"

"If you don't keep me up at least a couple more hours, I'll be sad."

He chuckled. "Your wish is my pleasure, sunshine."

"Thank you, jellyfish."

The incubus laughed. "Maybe I will get you that encyclopedia."

Giggling as he carried me to the bedroom, I conceded that maybe I needed to pick a different style of pet name. But we'd have plenty of time to figure it out tomorrow or the day after.

CHAPTER 14

Price

"This isn't so bad." Perl's breath fogged on the last word as the residual heat from the abrupt transfer left her. She doubled over, gasping, teeth chattering. "Never mind."

I'd forgotten how bloody cold it was in Hell.

I stalked over to Perl and put my hand on her shoulder, doing my best to transfer my warming spell so she would not freeze to death. Fortunately, being in Hell and many of my powers originating from demonic energy, my ability to do reliable magic was better down here.

Perl straightened after a moment with one last convulsive shiver. "What did you do?" She rubbed her hands together and resumed her perusal of our current circumstances.

"Magic," I replied curtly, and glanced around. "What the fuck did you do to my portal? It's supposed to be permanent. Hell, even Mayhem isn't here."

"We didn't do anything."

I didn't believe her, but somehow the portal had gotten redirected. I'd had no idea that was possible. I ran my hand through the longer part of my hair and sighed. "Okay, so here's the thing. We're going to be attacked. Maybe challenged first, maybe just attacked. I don't actually know how demons go about challenging someone to combat. Apparently, they're really excited about the idea of fighting me. So, maybe this was something one of them did. Anyway. Just keep your eyes open while I try to get us out of here."

The first thing I did was mentally shout for Inferno and Mayhem. Then, I tried to open my own portal.

It didn't work.

Fuck.

I kicked a rock before picking a direction and stomping away from Perl. Staying in one place wasn't a great idea, either.

She hurried to catch up. "Can't you portal us out of here?"

"I should be able to. My powers work better here since, essentially, I'm channeling demonic energy. Please don't ask."

She snapped her mouth shut, apparently content to do what I said for a change.

"But for some reason, they're not. They've been a little unstable since we defeated Mammon, but I don't usually have issues in Hell. I called for my Nightstallion. He'll hopefully be here soon. If I really have to, I'll give a shout for friends, but I'd rather just get back to Ezra's stronghold on my own."

"Who's Ezra?"

"The demon prince who owns the stronghold where my portal goes. He's a friend." I was annoyed enough that I wasn't even amused by my understatement.

"So, this is Hell," she mused after an extended silence.

"Part of it, anyway."

"How much of Hell have you seen?"

I sighed again. "Way more of it than I'd prefer. I was actually the ruler of Hell for a really short time. Not too many people outside of all the demons and angels know that. Which, I guess, that's a lot of beings, but not a lot of humans."

"That seems unlikely."

I shrugged. "Don't care if you believe me, mate. Just rambling while we wander."

"We need to rescue Gael and Becca."

"You're welcome to go and rescue them." I held my hands out to my sides and spun in a circle before continuing my trek. "Be my guest."

"Price!"

"What do you want me to do? I'm working on getting us someplace safer than where we are. Once I can actually make a portal or my nightstallion shows up, we'll go to safety." Well, if Inferno was willing to carry Perl, which I wasn't going to bet on. I had no idea why I was so reluctant to call on Lucifer to get me out of this.

Well...

I gave Perl some side-eye. I knew why. If I had been alone, I wouldn't have hesitated.

The prickling on the back of my neck was the only warning I had before the ground in front of me exploded in a spray of rock and sand. I managed to throw up a shield in time to keep the worst of it from hitting us.

Perl shouted in anger.

Glancing back, I noted the gun in her hand, glad it wasn't pointed at me. Still, if she hit the shield...

"Holster that, for now," I ordered. "The shield I threw up will send those bullets right back at us, and if one of them comes near me, it'll make it that much worse."

Perl reluctantly holstered the weapon in an ankle holster I really should have noticed before now.

Before I could continue, a creature rose from the ground, dirt cascading off its body.

Inadvertently, I shivered. This one must be some sort of nightmare demon, or something. If such things existed. It was the color of sand, had the head of a great white shark, complete with a dorsal fin on its back and pectoral fins, as if it swam through the dirt. But it stood on two feet and had arms in addition to fins. Its neck bent at an impossible angle for a shark, allowing it to stand upright and grin at us, showing a frightening amount of triangle teeth and reminding me of childhood fears. Especially after all the movies featuring killer sharks.

Living in the desert, I simply didn't have to worry about that, so shark attacks hadn't crossed my mind in ages. That made the fear all that much fresher, I supposed.

Mastering myself, I turned my glare on the demon. It was just a demon. Not some sort of actual crazy shark that could hurt me.

I realized that reassuring myself by thinking of something as just a demon was fucked up, but, well, it worked. Somewhat.

It sauntered? Yeah, sauntered was the right word. How a twenty-foot-tall demon shaped like a shark could saunter was beyond me, but it managed.

Perl swore.

I put my hands on my hips and added as much force in my voice as I could manage. "What is the meaning of this!"

The shark demon's smile widened, revealing rows and rows of teeth. "Price, we challenge you to a duel."

"We?" I made the mistake of asking.

While I'd been focused on the shark, more demons had joined us. I was getting sloppy. I hadn't noticed them right away. Or magic had prevented me for some reason.

A variety of the creatures seethed around us, more than I could count.

"Price." Perl's voice cracked.

"It'll be okay." And it would. Demons, I could handle. Even a fuckton of them. "The terms of the challenge?"

That seemed to take the demon aback. "Terms?"

"Usually in a challenge, there are rules."

"This is Hell, Price. No rules."

"Okay, great!" I wasn't completely surprised.

I left the protection of the shields, gesturing for Perl to stay behind.

Then, I let them attack me.

The wave of energy that pulsed out from my personal wards would have knocked me on my ass if it hadn't spread out evenly in all directions. As it was, it nearly knocked the wind out of me.

I staggered, but what shocked me more was the devastation around me. It was as if I were the center of a crater, and all that remained was the shield I'd thrown up around Perl, and a wall of sand blocking the horizon from view.

Perl was staring, slack jawed.

In the distance I heard a roar. Were they cheering or angry? Probably cheering.

The amount of energy I'd just thrown out staggered even me. I sucked in a few deep breaths and prepared for the next assault. I knew we weren't done. This time, instead of attacking me all at once, they hit in waves, hoping to overwhelm my wards.

It would work. Eventually. Every hit pulled energy, but it also sapped my strength. My original wards had used my personal energy to protect me and were easily overwhelmed. My demons had tied my new wards into a well of energy that was inexhaustible. That didn't mean I couldn't be overwhelmed if I wasn't careful.

I crafted another set of shields around myself just as the next wave of demons ran over the ridge of sand the blast had created. Demons of all sorts roared, cheered, screamed, and otherwise made a racket as they raced toward me. I swear a few of them were betting. Something was exchanging hands, anyway. One demon, skin a sickly yellow with spikes that dripped green liquid hammered its chest and roared at the sky. Fangs, blackened with rot, dripped the same green ichor. Ew. A few fliers with leathery wings circled above.

The sky overhead crackled and arcs of electricity spread fingers across the sky. The air smelled dry and dusty with an edge of ozone from the lightning arching across the sky.

That gave me an idea. Focusing for a moment, I pulled the ground underneath me and Perl higher, leaving a donut-shaped ring around us that I summoned water into. My powers really did work so much better down here.

The water slowly filled the depression just as the first demons reached it. They splashed into the donut of liquid, and I called the electricity from the sky.

The resulting electrocution was not something I ever wanted to witness again. Many of the demons simply died, some leaving bodies, some dissipating into smoke or goo. Others must have had some resistance to lightning and screamed, thrashed, and cooked in their skin.

The smell was horrific, burned hair and entrails and charred meat. I gagged before I threw up a magical filter for the stench.

"Okay, that was a terrible idea," I choked out, apparently just loud enough for Perl to hear.

"But effective," she pointed out, from where she sheltered behind the shields I'd erected, again clutching her gun.

I declined to reply.

The remaining demons regrouped on the other side of the moat I'd built for us.

A crack of light split the air next to me, and someone I had hoped not to run into stepped out. Not because I didn't want to see the ruler of Hell. No, I just didn't want him and Perl to interact.

"What in the nine hells is going on here?" Lucifer's voice boomed out.

The shark-bodied demon who had somehow survived the onslaught came forward and bowed.

"My liege, we didn't train hard enough. We will correct that error."

Lucifer stared, flabbergasted for a moment before he waved his hand at the demons. "Get out of my sight."

The demons scattered, leaving the three of us alone in the crater.

"Chris, what the fuck?"

"They wanted to fight and somehow redirected my portal from Ezra's. That's all I know. Sabian and Mayhem went through before us and hopefully ended up with Ezra."

Lucifer pinched the bridge of his nose, and I couldn't help admiring his powerful form. Tall, muscular, and mine... My desire for him flared, especially since we'd been denied already a few times. Despite his irritation, I wanted to climb him like a tree.

His lips quirked into a smile. He knew what was on my mind.

"Who's your friend?"

"Uh, this is Perl. Apparently, some of your demons ran off with a couple of her fellow hunters along with some chaps from the Vatican, and I told her I'd see if I could get them back. She decided to join me at the last minute." I made a face and let him see a quick memory of my transit through the portal.

Lucifer turned his full terrifying charm onto Perl. She lifted her chin and unconsciously smoothed her hair, though she paled considerably. She was smart enough to holster her gun, again.

"I regret my intrusion," she said with a stiff nod. She had to have guessed who it was she faced.

"I'm rather sure you do." Lucifer let his gaze roam her body. "Well, let's retrieve your friends and get you out of my realm."

Even I hadn't expected it to be that easy. Perl shot me an uneasy glance. "Is it safe?" she whispered.

I snorted, but otherwise didn't answer.

Lucifer opened another portal, and I followed him through. Perl, wisely, chose to join us.

We stepped out into his throne room.

"Any idea how they managed to redirect a permanent portal?" I had been here enough that I barely glanced around. Perl was gawking like a tourist. I couldn't blame her.

"I'm not entirely certain it was the demons that did that. It was actually more likely a secondary protection in the portal itself that dumped you out on the Azoth plane. It's keyed to specific people, yet someone else found a way to slip through the entrance, so it may have reacted by sending you somewhere unexpected."

"That makes more sense than a bunch of lesser demons figuring out how to redirect one of your portals. Cool. So, what now?"

"We retrieve Perl's friends and send them away, and you and I discuss the price of my assistance."

He winked before Perl could bring her attention back to us.

"Sir, it was my doing. I should be the one to pay the price." Her voice was tight, but full of conviction.

Since I knew what Lucifer wanted, I was more amused than worried about her safety. In another life, I might have been figuring out a way to negotiate for our release. Now, I was more than happy to go along with the game.

"Ahh, but it was Chris who failed to safeguard her portal. That requires its own punishment." He stepped over to me, tracing a finger along my jaw and arcing electric pleasure through my skin.

Perl gave me a wide-eyed look.

I shrugged, not up to pretending much concern and trying to hide my reaction to his touch.

Just then, Inferno made an appearance. I wasn't sure where he'd come from, but he raced into the throne room, mane, tail, and feathers on his legs fully alight with demonic flame. His hooves pounded on the stone before he skidded to a halt in front of Lucifer and reared, pawing the air inches from the fallen angel's face.

If this was something they had planned, I wasn't in on it. Lucifer didn't move, didn't even seem surprised.

"Inferno, knock it off," I snapped. "We're guests."

The nightstallion put all four hooves on the ground, but continued to snort and paw, before backing up until he was at my side. Mayhem chose that moment to pop into existence in full flaming hellhound fury.

I turned my attention back to Lucifer in time to catch the flash of a bemused expression on his face before he schooled it back to impassiveness.

Perl scrambled back from the nightstallion. "What the hell?"

"Nightstallion," I said tersely. She already knew Mayhem was a hellhound.

Before she could question me further, a very classic-looking demon walked in dragging two humans. Classic if you were talking TV imagery, anyway. Tall, cloven hooved, thick bull horns off his head. He bowed to me before dropping Becca and Gael at my feet like an offering.

He clomped off before I could think of what to say.

The two hunters looked a little worse for wear, but not really damaged physically. I suspected their mental wounds would take a bit longer to heal. Getting them out of here would help a lot.

I glanced up at Lucifer. He studied us before waving his hand. This portal was a bit grander, with blue flames flickering at the edges, just barely visible.

After a side-eyed glance at Lucifer, I gestured for Perl and her friends to go.

Becca and Gael struggled to their feet with our help. Perl shook her head.

"Really, the fault is mine. I should pay the price."

Lucifer smiled, and I stepped between them, putting my hands out on either side before he could get snarky or otherwise require some payment. We had enough to deal with right now.

"Go!"

Perl followed my order and they left.

Belatedly, I thought to ask where the portal was sending them, as it snapped shut on her heels.

"Please tell me that sent them somewhere not awful."

The devil chuckled. "You didn't specify and neither did they. I sent them to the Vatican. Tweak their noses a little."

I sighed. "Okay, well, that's nice. What about the others that your demons picked up."

"Leave the inquisitors to me."

The tone in his voice made that final, and I didn't push. I didn't really care that much.

"So, about my price." His amused smile turned into something panty melting.

I licked my lips in anticipation.

Inferno stomped his hoof and Mayhem growled.

"What's wrong, buddy?" I put my hand on his shoulder and had a thought. "Hey, thanks for coming for me. When I shouted for help, I was facing a bunch of demons, not Lucifer." I opened myself to him through the bond and showed him the memory, in case he was confused about what had happened earlier.

Inferno shook his head, but his fires dimmed, and he nuzzled me. That must have been it. He'd never had a problem with Lucifer before. Mayhem also calmed.

"Well, I guess it's good to know he'll fight even you for me if he thinks he needs to," I said, hugging my fiery mount.

Lucifer came over to us and held out his hand for Inferno to investigate. The nightstallion accepted a treat I hadn't noticed then blew gently on the demon's hand. Accepting him again now that he knew Lucifer hadn't been a threat.

I gave my mount one more pat then turned my attention back to my demon.

"Well, my exorcist, shall we?"

"I've been denied too long." I tugged on his arm. "Let's go."

He took my hand and kissed my knuckles. "Anything for you, my dear. Anything."

Dakota Brown

CHAPTER 15

Price

"I thought you'd at least pretend to make it difficult to get the hunters away."

Lucifer shrugged. "I didn't want to start a fight with Inferno. Besides, they weren't supposed to be in Hell. We were only after the inquisitors. The demons occasionally have a hard time telling who's who on the mortal plane."

I shuddered at the thought. "What on earth is going on?"

He shrugged again. "We're working on it, love."

I let the devil distract me with his charming grin and his intense gaze as he led me from the throne room to his private chamber. With a wave of his hand, a blaze started in the fireplace.

His private rooms were extensive. The one he liked best was a large study of sorts just off his bedroom. Yes, the Devil does have a bedroom, but he doesn't necessarily need sleep the same way a human does. Usually only when he's been injured. Though he's never seemed to mind sleeping with me just for the experience.

I sank down into one of the comfortable armchairs by the door and undid the laces on my boots. One of the things I really liked about the room was the plush carpet, best experienced barefoot.

The walls were stone, as if the entire room had been carved from a solid rock. I wasn't even entirely certain that it hadn't been. The furniture was all heavy dark wood with deep cushions and extraordinarily comfortable.

My absolute favorite thing about the room was the pile of furs in front of the fireplace. As an exorcist, I couldn't make myself feel bad about some demon or another who had displeased Lucifer and gotten turned into a rug. I might have objected if they were animal furs. These were as soft as mink but environmentally friendly. I curled my toes in the fur and stared into the fire. My devil came up behind me and pulled me close, his arms wrapped around me, his chest pressed against my back.

"My dear, are you quite all right?"

I shivered as his lips pressed against my neck.

"I will be. This whole thing with the hunters and the inquisition is troublesome. The vampire creature they're hunting is even more troublesome." I hunched my shoulders.

His fingers dug into my shoulders, easing some of the tension away. "Not even worried about having to fight all those demons?"

"Eh, mate, that's like, old hat at this point. And it mostly only impacts me. This other stuff though… well who knows what is going to happen."

He kissed my neck again. "I'll have someone look into it, love. For now, let's forget about all of that."

More than willing to let him take me away from my worries for a little while, I took a deep breath and relaxed into his touch.

"What would you like from me tonight?" he murmured.

"Your choice."

"As you wish." His voice lowered to even more seductive levels as he traced his fingers down my sides, before hooking them in the hem of my shirt.

I lifted my arms as he pulled my shirt upward. The slide of his fingers against my skin ignited sparks that spiraled through me. I released the last of the tension from my body and surrendered to my fallen angel.

He wrapped his fingers around my wrists and held my hands aloft. Soft cords wrapped around my wrists and arms. I glanced up in time to see black silk sliding down my skin and binding my arms above my head. Demon magic at its finest.

Lucifer's warm hands left trails of heat on my sides. He unhooked my bra then rumbled in displeasure as he realized his mistake.

Before I could offer any sort of suggestion, it disappeared, reappearing on the floor by my shirt.

Lucifer traced his fingers along the pathway he, Mal, and Brennan had created on my body for the wards that kept me safe. My skin sparked as he applied just enough force to almost trigger them. It sent electric thrills arcing through my body.

Gasping, I trembled at the hint of pain along with the pleasure. My skin dampened with sweat as my arousal grew.

"These truly were a fun addition." Lucifer skirted danger by applying just a touch more power.

I went to my toes as the power flooded through me, ready to shove the devil away but not quite over the threshold. My vision swam as I floated on the energy racing through my system. It was nearly as good as an orgasm.

"Yeah, you're about to get thrown across the room," I warned, my voice thick with lust.

"Am I?"

I'd shut my eyes, but I could picture the grin on his face from the tone of his voice.

He walked his fingers down my stomach until he reached the button on my jeans. He popped that open and slowly lowered the zipper.

"How does your kinky vampire get away with his games then?"

"He is more careful." I opened my eyes to see the endless depths and burning hellfire in Lucifer's.

"I'm perfectly careful."

Before I could reply, he took another length of black silk and tied it around my eyes.

"You may always tell me no," he murmured in my ear.

I let the blindfold stay. "I know."

He slid my pants down, then carefully lifted each leg to get them off, massaging my foot for a moment while it was in the air. After setting my wards alight with practiced strokes of his fingers, he nudged my feet apart.

I was startled when his tongue flicked across my folds. Lucifer didn't get on his knees for anyone. Anyone but me. I almost wished I could see the pretty sight of the devil on his knees worshiping at my dripping altar.

Moaning as he applied his tongue and lips to my clit, I shuddered, grateful the magical silken bindings were holding me upright as my legs gave out.

I cried out as an orgasm ripped through me.

Lucifer didn't let me rest, though, sliding a finger inside me and stroking me back to near explosion.

"You're so wet," he murmured. "Ready to take me."

"Mmhm," I agreed, hoping he would cage himself inside me right then.

Instead, he joined his first finger with a second, stroking from the inside and lapping at my folds and clit from the outside until I was practically screaming his name and squirming in my bonds.

"I do like it when you scream. Now come for me."

I thrust against his fingers and my body shattered into a million pieces of ecstasy. Sweat drenched my skin, and my muscles felt like I'd been running from demons for hours.

Instead, I edged toward this demon.

"Now?"

"Mmm, maybe," he trailed fingers along my stomach, teasing me.

I heard the rustle of cloth before he pressed his bare chest against mine. "Maybe you should come a few more times first."

I lost count of the number of times he made me come before he finally thrust himself inside me.

Groaning with pleasure, I opened to take him as deeply as I could. Lucifer lifted my hips, and I wrapped my legs around his waist.

"Fuck, that feels so damn good," I gasped out as he pounded into me.

"Yes, my love, it does." His voice had lost the smoothness, the practiced charm, and fallen into a rough lust that just turned me on more. It wasn't everyone who could undo the devil like that. Just me and I loved it.

He was deep inside me when I shattered again, and his shout of pleasure as he stiffened let me know my timing was perfect.

"I want to see you."

He slipped the blindfold off my face. Sweat plastered his hair to his face, and the hellfire dancing in the depths of his eyes seemed extra bright. His lips met mine, and, still impaled on his cock and hanging from magical ties, I lost myself in his kiss.

"I thought I should make up for lost time," he finally said, helping me down and rubbing my arms as the magical bonds vanished.

I didn't have words, unsteady on my feet. I collapsed to my knees in front of him—and took his semi hard cock in my mouth.

He sucked in a breath, and it didn't take much to get him hard again. I hummed as I worked my lips along his length.

"Fuck," he breathed, eyes shuttering and a look of complete surrender crossing his face.

I watched until his hands were shaking on my shoulders.

"Chris," he warned.

I grunted acknowledgement and kept going until he spilled in my mouth as I swallowed, continuing to suck until he dug his fingers into my shoulders.

Then I released him and fell back to the soft furs, watching as the firelight played across the planes of his muscles until he collapsed beside me.

"Guess I had a little time to make up for, too."

"Yes, an excellent reminder that I should never let business get between my cock and your marvelous pussy."

I snorted laughter and curled up into his arms. "We have a little time. Let's remind each other some more."

With a laugh, the devil rolled me onto my back and traced his finger between my breasts.

"A fine idea, my dearest exorcist. A fine idea, indeed."

CHAPTER 16

Price

I was in an uncommonly good mood when I showed up to help open the pizza shop the next day. At least three of the hunters were out of the country, and Asher was heading for the airport with passports for his friends. I hopefully wouldn't have to deal with them again for a while.

This vampire they were hunting still hadn't popped up, and I was happy to leave it to Lucifer and the hunters. Mal and Sabian were off at his occult shop with Olivia, his co-owner, doing inventory. I'd rather spin dough.

Aaron was at work. I knew he was making it back to the house most nights. He mostly just grabbed whatever was in the fridge and passed out. Except the other night when I'd had my way with him. That memory warmed me, and I hoped we could do it again, soon.

I wasn't sure where Brennan was, and Ezra was whelping a litter of hellhounds. I couldn't wait to meet them. Mayhem trotted around in his fluffy Pomeranian shape, doing his best impression of an invisible dog. One of the many advantages of having a hellhound. He didn't shed, so I didn't feel bad letting him in the kitchen.

Not to mention, I couldn't wait until Billy got in. I had a surprise for him. I just hoped it wasn't too soon.

Puttering around the rebuilt pizza parlor before my employees arrived was peaceful. The wards lent a heavy stillness to the place that melded with the leftover chaos from hundreds of patrons. We'd been slammed almost every night since we officially reopened. The wood stove was hugely popular, too, and I congratulated myself on a good decision.

Briefly, I wondered how my parents would feel about the changes I'd made to the place. They'd been killed almost six years ago now, by a demon I'd recently destroyed. I'd blamed myself for their deaths, and I probably always would feel at least partially responsible. I now knew there had been other things going on that had led to this particular demon seeking me out. It hadn't been my fault, but a couple of former friends who had fucked around with summoning demons then turned one loose on me because I wouldn't stay to protect them from their mistakes.

The bell chimed and Billy walked in. Perfect.

"Hi, boss."

"Hi, Billy." I set the cup I'd been inspecting on the counter and gestured toward the office.

He followed, eyebrow raising slightly. "World ending?"

"Naw."

We reached the office, and I opened the door. "Now, if it's too soon, just let me know and I'll tell her to wait, but if it's okay, I brought this up for you."

An open box sat on my desk. Billy tilted his head, curious.

"What?"

At his voice, a tawny head with black-tipped, tufted ears popped up. The wide, slitted green eyes focused in on him, and she gave a demanding meow.

Billy's jaw dropped, and he stared. After a moment, he shot me a sidelong glance. "You said up?"

"Uh, yeah, she's a hellcat."

"No strings attached?"

I smiled. "You've been hanging around me too much. Smart question. No, no strings. A gift from someone who wishes to remain nameless, but shouldn't be hard to guess, for services rendered."

The hellcat meowed again.

"And if you had asked me a year ago if I'd be happily giving out creatures from Hell, well... I'd have probably punched you. So, enjoy that irony."

Billy smiled but didn't actually laugh. He just went forward and held out his hands. The hellcat rose up out of the box and allowed him to pick her up. She immediately started a rumble that I could feel in my soul and pushed her head up against his chin. She appeared to be a Savanna cat, except for the tuft ears.

Billy started sobbing into her fur. I wasn't surprised. It was soon to be offering him a new cat, but sometimes that's what you needed.

"You can say no."

"She's perfect. Just, uh, give me a few minutes," he managed to get out.

"Take all the time you need, Billy. I'll handle things up front. She's a lot like Mayhem. Intelligent, shape shifter, etc. But she's yours. Make sure you name her right away to complete the bond."

He nodded, face still buried in her fur. The hellcat was now somewhat draped over his shoulder, and she kneaded his back, kindly keeping her claws in check.

I left them alone, hating to make Billy cry but thinking it was likely the right move to get him this new friend. He spent too much time alone as it was.

Others had filtered in by the time I made it back into the kitchen, starting the process of getting ready for the day. I lost myself in the routine, sparing a brief glance for

Billy as he finally joined us, with his cat riding on his shoulder.

She hopped down before he got to the kitchen and found a pile of merchandise shirts to make a bed on.

I shook my head. Cats...

Mayhem trotted over to the stack and stared up at her. The cat stared down.

"Both of you behave," I ordered.

They both glanced at me. Mayhem with a wag of his fluffy tail, the cat with a look that said I wasn't the boss of her.

"I may not be the boss of you, but this is my shop, and I can literally kick you out, hellcat or not. Behave."

She turned her attention from me and the hellhound, sitting with her back turned, licking one paw. I took that for cat-like assent and turned my attention back to opening the parlor.

It wasn't until our front door chimed and our first customer was waiting at the hostess stand that any of us noticed Mandy wasn't here. I quickly got the person seated, had Rebecca take over the hostess duties, and went back to the office.

"Billy, did Mandy call out?"

"No." He frowned and dug out his cell phone. He stared at the screen before unlocking it and making a call.

He glanced up at me, a frown creasing his brow. "It went to voicemail."

"Fuck. That's not like her."

I tried and got the same results. Not that I had expected her to answer me if she was actively ignoring Billy. One last try. I called Mal.

"Hey, Mal. Can Sabian contact Warrick somehow on like incubus cellular or something? Mandy didn't show up and she's not answering her phone."

Mal swore. "Call you back."

I waited silently with Billy until my phone chimed.

"Sabian says Warrick is missing from every sense he has on this side of things. We're heading back to the house now and he'll pop over to Ezra's place and check from there."

"Great." I hung up and ran my hand through my hair. "Fuck." This might call for that locate spell I'd used what seemed like a lifetime ago to find Mal. Though I'd been looking for something else entirely.

"Go," Billy said. "I'll handle shit here."

"Call me the minute she shows up or you hear from her." I already knew she wasn't going to show up, though. Mandy going missing was one thing. Emergencies happened and phones were only as good as their batteries, but if Sabian couldn't locate Warrick, that was weird and worrisome. The demon wouldn't have let anything happen to Mandy if he could stop it, but incubi were notoriously bad in a fight, so if something supernatural had come after them, he likely wouldn't have been a lot of help. Anything human, he could have handled easily.

I hurried out of the pizza shop, not taking the time to say anything to my employees and swung my leg over the Harley-shaped nightstallion. Mayhem followed close behind.

Inferno shifted and launched into the air. The quick trip back to my place was a blur, and I leaped off his back as soon as we touched down and sprinted for the house. Sabian was coming up the stairs from the basement portal when I burst in. Mal on his heels.

The expression on his face was all I needed.

"Locater spell?"

Mal frowned then nodded, turned, and headed back into the basement. Sabian and I followed, though the incubus took a moment to give me a quick hug and a kiss on the forehead.

By the time we were down there, Mal had already set up the spell likely using his vampire quickness.

Though I didn't want to get rusty with my skills, Mal had used a slightly different setup than I was used to, so I didn't try to get involved. His spell might even be less fickle than mine. I could hope, anyway.

Mal said a few words, snuffed the candle, and held up a pendulum. It leaned unerringly toward the north.

"Huh. There's not much north of here."

"Not directly north of us, no," Mal agreed. "Road trip?"

"Looks like." I rubbed my arms with my hands, not quite sure what made me think she wasn't close, but Mal agreed.

"I'll grab some things for us," Sabian offered.

Mal glanced at the incubus then at me. "Sabian, maybe you should stay behind."

He frowned then his eyes widened. "Ahh." He turned his amber eyes on me, and I could sense his indecision.

"Mal may be right." I twisted my lips. "As much as I hate to leave you behind, it might be better if you stayed and helped Olivia and Billy. I'm not saying you would be useless, but if you're in any sort of extra danger because of this, well…" I sighed.

"No, I get it. I can stay. Take Brennan though. He's handy in a fight."

Mal nodded and pulled out his phone.

"I will grab things for you three," Sabian said and left.

Through our bond, I could feel his conflict. A touch of relief at not having to face another fight, and guilt at letting me go without him. Not wanting him to feel bad, I followed.

"Hey," I said when I caught up. "You are helping by keeping an eye on things here."

He took a breath and nodded, some of the tension easing from his muscular shoulders. "I know. It's still hard."

I wrapped my arms around him from behind and pressed my cheek against his back. "I love you, Sabian. This is okay. If we need backup, we'll call, and you and Ezra can come to the rescue. And maybe Aaron if we need an angel."

Sabian clasped his hand around mine and squeezed gently. "It's a plan, love. Okay, let me get you three packed. Brennan isn't far away, and he'll be here soon. You'll have to talk Inferno into becoming an SUV or something."

I chuckled but worry kept me from much mirth.

And this morning had started out so good.

Fuck.

Dakota Brown

CHAPTER 17

Mandy

I stared out into the night, letting the hot water bake me as the steam rose from the surface of the liquid. I blinked a few times. Where was I? Why was I in a hot tub?

Warrick sat across from me, also staring into the distance. He was wearing his clothing. In the hot tub. Weird.

Glancing down, I saw I was also wearing my clothing.

What the hell?

I started to overheat. The discomfort brought about panic, and I struggled out of the water and flopped on the ground like a drowned fish. Where I immediately regretted my life choice. I hadn't noticed the snow until I was planted face first in it. My body wasn't responding right and though I managed to get to my feet, I stood there, swaying. I'd been wearing my shoes, too. Everything was soaked, and the air was frigid and sucked the breath from my lungs.

Shivering violently and hyperventilating, I tried to get my bearings. Santa Fe certainly got cold in the winter, and we even saw snow now and again, but nothing like this. The white blanket reflected the moon as far as I could see.

Where the hell was I?

Before I could freeze, warm arms wrapped around me.

"Mandy?" Warrick sounded as confused as I felt.

"We have to get warm," I stammered.

The incubus dragged me back into the hot tub.

A quiet lassitude tried to intrude upon my mind. I pushed it away, too freaked out to give in to the feeling.

"Is this hot tub literally in the middle of nowhere?"

Warrick twisted me by the shoulders until I could see behind us. Why hadn't I thought to look behind us?

A long, low building that looked like a horror movie hotel stretched behind us. Beyond was a parking lot full of semi-trucks and trailers and a gas station obviously built to accommodate the large vehicles.

"A truck stop?" My brain was starting to work a little faster, and the questions kept piling up. None of this made sense.

Warrick shuddered. "There is a very large blank in my memory. The last thing I recall, we were hiking in the desert."

"This is certainly not the desert."

Warrick nodded grimly.

I started to overheat again. "We need to get inside and out of these clothes."

The incubus felt in his pockets under the water. "I have a room key." He pulled out an old-fashioned key with a number on it.

"That's so weird. Fuck, I hope there aren't bedbugs." Probably the least of my worries right now.

He shuddered but held out a hand and assisted me out of the hot tub. Then we sprinted to the hotel. Fortunately, we were on the first floor, and it didn't take long to find our room. Or at least the room we had a key to. My hair was already freezing, and my clothing was stiff with cold by the time Warrick shoved the door open and dragged me inside.

It was warm in the room, and I stood there, shivering. Once my eyeballs were defrosted, I glanced around. It was a standard two bed, with a bathroom off to the side. It was small, crowded, and yellowed. The hint of smoke in the air wrinkled my nose. Despite that, it seemed like it had a chance of being clean.

The beds were made with clean white sheets. One bed was occupied. The other was rumpled but not gross.

The occupant of the other bed didn't move.

Warrick pulled me past the beds and into the tiny bathroom. He locked the door and we stripped and warmed back up in the shower to hopefully avoid hypothermia. I wanted to know who the other person in the room was. Getting warm had been the priority, though.

Then he applied a bit of magic and dried our clothing.

"Bless you," I murmured.

Warrick snorted.

"Uh, sorry."

He waved away my concerns. "Simply amusing. I would have done it sooner, but nothing was working. I still feel fuzzy and disconnected."

"So, what's going on?" We hadn't spoken while we cleaned up.

"I have no idea." Warrick shifted uneasily. "This is easily the weirdest thing that has ever happened to me, and I've spent much of my life in Hell."

"Yeah. Same. Well… not same, but same."

He cast me a faint smile before putting his hand on the doorknob. After a quick glance at me, to which I nodded, he unlocked the door and opened it.

We went out into the main room.

The person in the other bed hadn't moved.

"Uh, hello," I squeaked out.

Clearing my throat, I tried again, louder.

No response.

Warrick went over and pulled back the sheets.

I clapped my hand over my mouth to stifle a scream.

A body lay in the bed. A body with a shaft of wood through its chest, and a bloodstain on the shirt. Though there didn't seem to be enough blood for the type of wound. The man had sandy blond hair. He was probably tall, but slender where Warrick was a little bulkier.

"Well, I don't think he's dead," Warrick said after a moment, perhaps oblivious to my horror.

"What?!"

"Vampire." Warrick shrugged, then glanced at me, his eyes going wide. He came over and wrapped me in a hug.

"Why is there a staked vampire in our room?"

"Why is any of this happening?" Warrick shuddered. "I have exactly no answers."

I was about to break into sobs when someone knocked on the door.

Hurriedly, I swallowed them down.

This night just kept getting better. What the hell was going on?

Warrick scooted me behind him before he went to open the door.

I had no idea what to expect, but a blank eyed human-shaped something was not it. And by blank eyed, I meant blank white orbs where normal eyeballs might have otherwise been. The being was a man. He stood stiffly and stared straight ahead.

"Hello?" Warrick finally prompted.

The being's arm rose from his side, stiff, like his shoulder was a hinge and his hand was on a string being pulled up to chest level. In his hand was a piece of paper.

After a moment, Warrick took it.

The being's arm lowered, and he turned and walked off, moving rapidly but unsteadily away.

"What the hell?"

Warrick slammed the door shut, turned the bolt, and slid the locking chain into place before studying the paper in his hand.

"I'm almost afraid to look," he admitted.

"Does it have any magic on it?" His concerns were valid on multiple levels. I certainly shared them.

"Not that I can sense, but my powers are still fidgety." Warrick took a deep breath then unfolded the paper.

Do not wake the vampire.

The handwriting was eloquent, with extravagant curls and flourishes like you might see in an old manuscript.

"Keeps getting weirder." I shuddered and glanced back at the body in the bed.

Warrick ran his hand through his dark hair and sighed. "It's either a very clever ploy to get us to wake the bastard up, or it's an actual command that is supposed to be backed by magic but somehow the magic isn't working? Or, you know, something else that I can't figure out right now. We're not in some sort of weird live action murder mystery, are we?"

"I wish. Wait!" I patted my pockets. Nothing. My momentary elation dimmed a little when I couldn't find my phone. Searching the room produced the same results. "Well, shit. Never mind."

"Yeah, I don't know where our phones are. Or why we're getting secret messages from zombies, or why we're in the middle of wherever the hell we are with a staked vampire." The incubus curled in on himself and seemed on the verge of a breakdown.

I knew how he felt.

"You can't get a hold of Sabian or anyone, can you? With your powers?"

Warrick shook his head. "Still fuzzy, or they're being blocked."

"Cool," I muttered, feeling anything but calm. "So, do we wake this guy up and see if he has answers? Mal said most vampires are dicks."

"We can feed him my blood. That will give me something of an 'in' as it were into his mind, and I can probably control him enough for us to re-stake him if he's too crazy."

"Ahh, sure?"

"I agree it's not the best idea. But it is the only one I have. I really think this note is supposed to carry some form of command with it. It's just not working anymore." Warrick went over to the bed and poked the vampire on the shoulder. "Yeah, definitely unconscious, but alive. I can feel his energy. Much shallower than Mal. This is a pretty young vampire."

"You know Mal is older than dirt, right? If you're comparing to him, this could still be an old, powerful vampire."

Warrick nodded. "I agree, my estimate could be off, but at least we're not dealing with a vampire anywhere close to as powerful as Mal."

"Okay, valid. How do we do this?" I forged ahead with the idea because if I thought about it too long, I'd realize how dumb this was. But also, what choice did we have? Well, we had a few. None of them good. And the vampire could be a potential ally, depending on why he had gotten staked in the first place. And what had Warrick and I done to be involved with all this? And what was *this* anyway?

"I'll shove my wrist in his mouth. You pull the stake out."

The incubus got himself into position, and I grabbed the thick end of the stake protruding from the guy's chest. My hands shook, and I avoided looking at the vampire.

"Go ahead." Warrick held the vampire, his wrist near the other man's throat and a worried pinch to his brow.

"This is a terrible idea," I said as I yanked.

The body jerked, but the stake barely moved.

I shrieked and dropped the stake, jumping backward.

"Mandy, just a little harder." Warrick put a soothing hand on my shoulder and gently guided me back to the prone vampire.

"Maybe you should pull it out."

"I need to be able to guarantee he bites me instead of you. You have to do it."

Shaking my head violently in objection, I reached out to try again. I did not want to do this.

My fingers trembled and my limbs turned to jelly as I once again grasped the rough wood and pulled.

It was stuck.

"Um, maybe like put your foot on his chest and use that to brace against."

I stared at Warrick for a moment to see if he was joking. When it was clear the incubus was serious, I climbed on the bed, put my foot on the vampire's chest, and yanked.

The stake gave, and I flailed and shrieked as I fell backward, bouncing once on the bed before tumbling to the floor.

My heart thudded in my chest, and I laid there, staring at the brown-stained ceiling for a while before remembering the danger Warrick was in, and I scrambled to my feet.

The vampire had Warrick's arm cradled in his hands, lips on the incubus' wrist. The expression on Warrick's face was one of happy bliss.

CHAPTER 18

Mandy

I watched the vampire and Warrick, dancing in place, not sure if I should interrupt or not. Warrick could handle a lot more than a human could. I bit my nails and tried to make myself go over to my lover and pull his wrist out of the vampire's mouth. I couldn't make myself get any closer and I cried out in frustration. This was all just too much.

The vampire released Warrick, and my incubus fell back on the bed, staring up at the ceiling with glazed eyes and a very obvious erection straining against his pants.

Well, we knew what a vampire's bite did, so it wasn't a surprise. I took a breath, trying to calm myself down. The sight of Warrick uninjured and obviously feeling good helped.

A rather embarrassingly large part of me got all sorts of hot and bothered by the sight, but the rest of me was more concerned with the vampire who now glanced around the room curiously, before his gaze settled on me.

"Where the bloody hell are we?"

My heart sank. If he didn't have any answers, what were we going to do? On the plus side, he wasn't trying to murder us, so yay? And his English accent was yummy. And I could see that his eyes were a light crystal blue now.

"You don't know?"

"Lady, I just woke up from a stake-induced nap in the most generic of hotel rooms in existence. The only thing I know is that I probably haven't been asleep until far in the future, but that's based more on how I feel than on the surroundings." He sounded worried, but not overly belligerent.

"What's the last date you remember?" Warrick slurred.

"Ahh, thanks for the assist, there." The vampire twisted to study Warrick, who still lay on the bed next to him. "Hmm, last date." He wrinkled his nose while he thought, and it was extremely adorable. After a minute of contemplation, during which I fidgeted and kept looking for a phone I didn't have to check the date, he named off something that wasn't too far from the last date I remembered.

"Probably only out a week or two, then," Warrick replied, sounding a little steadier. "We're not exactly sure when or where we are, either."

"No? Well, balls." He sighed. "I suppose we're not in Maine still?"

"I'm going to guess no," Warrick said. "But I could be wrong. We were in New Mexico before we woke up here."

"Ahh. Well, that's something." He frowned, then peered at Warrick. "Must still be waking up from the rude staking. I've never tasted blood like yours before."

"Incubus," Warrick slurred, still a little drunk on the high from the vampire's bite.

The vampire's eyes widened, and he scooted away from the demon.

"Dude, you're a vampire. I don't think you have too much to worry about," Warrick said, sitting up.

"Eh, right." He didn't seem comforted, though.

"Okay, so anyway, that's Warrick. I'm Mandy. What's your name?" My racing pulse calmed at the vampire's continued friendliness.

"Harrison."

"Nice to meet you, Harrison. So, we woke up in a hot tub in the middle of a snowstorm wearing all our clothing," I explained. "The last thing we remember before that was that we were on a hike together in the desert. Somehow, we ended up here. We also have no idea what is going on. Oh, and this zombie showed up and gave us a note telling us not to wake the vampire. So, of course, we woke you up." I hugged myself. "The entire situation is insane."

We were interrupted by another knock on the door.

A chill trickled down my spine and into my gut. We all stared at each other, none of us moving.

"The master requires the demon," a toneless voice said from the other side of the door. Obviously, the soundproofing was terrible.

We didn't dare speak, but Warrick's eyes widened further as he shook his head, before glancing around for an escape route.

"He's not here right now," I finally said.

"Then the human will do."

Shit. Still, my fear was less than Warrick's.

"Okay." And maybe we could find something out.

Warrick shook his head more frantically. I gestured for him to stay and headed for the door. I glanced around for a coat, remembering the cold, but didn't see one. Hopefully, we wouldn't be outside for too long.

Warrick tried to stand, but fell back on the bed, still clearly drained from Harrison's bite.

"Stay. It's okay." I waved him back, unchained and unbolted the door before slipping outside. The cold was like a punch to the gut, sucking the air out of my lungs and seizing up my muscles. Gasping, I shoved my arms into my armpits.

The being that waited reminded me of the zombie, except it was slightly more animate. The skin was stretched over the skull, the hair was thin and lank, and the eyes jaundiced. Its body was human shaped, but if a human skin had been stretched over bones and not stuffed with any organs. The thing wore clothing, but nothing appropriate for the weather. It barely regarded me before turning, probably expecting me to follow. I did because what else was I going to do?

At least I knew the supernatural existed. If I hadn't known, I'd have been losing my shit. As it was, I was still losing my shit, just not as badly. And somewhere, in the back of my mind, I knew Chris and Mal would be coming for me. That, more than anything, kept me going.

The zombie creature moved just fast enough that I thought I might not die of exposure before we got inside the hotel office, which is where we seemed to be headed.

I almost dashed ahead. Then restrained myself just in case I was supposed to be acting a certain way, or just going to the wrong place. It was a close thing, though. I was freezing and already couldn't feel my extremities. What was a zombie doing at a human hotel? Where the fuck were we?

When we reached the door, the zombie stood next to it. I used my sleeve to grab the door handle and rushed inside. Sure, whatever was on the other side was probably worse than freezing to death in the middle of wherever the hell we were. At that moment I didn't care.

The stench of stale cigarette smoke was overpowering, and I sneezed. Then the tremors hit, locking up my back and chattering my teeth. I'd been shivering outside, but something about being back in the warmth signaled to my body how cold I'd actually been. I tucked my hands in my armpits and studied my surroundings while I shivered.

The lobby looked, and smelled, like every dive hotel lobby I'd ever seen in person or in a movie. Yellowed ceiling, yellowed walls, a few cigarette burns on the chipped counter. The mingled smell of smoke and mildew was threatening to make me sneeze again.

"Human, where is the demon?"

"In the snow." It was the dumbest answer ever, but I had no idea what else to say and it just popped out. We had been out in the hot tub, after all.

"Ahh, well, you'll do. Get in here."

Wait, that made sense? This was so fucking weird.

I walked into the office behind the desk. A man? A what? What was he? Someone presenting as male and human sat behind the desk. His hair was black with a faint wave to it, and his skin was dusky, but yellowed like the ceiling above him. He wore a modern suit and tie. The fancy clothing in this environment was so out of place it was jarring. All I could do was stare, mouth slightly open.

The expression in his deep brown eyes when I briefly met them, though, snapped my jaw shut and had me backing away. They were absolutely devoid of any sort of humanity. He had flat eyes like a shark. Almost lifeless. The expression on his face was similarly shark like. No real emotion, just curiosity that could switch to hunger in a moment. How did I know that? Well, maybe that was a memory from the gap between home and here.

"Go and retrieve the motorized conveyance from the stable area. We will all be leaving soon."

The creature tossed a set of keys at me and turned away.

I wanted to demand an answer, find out what was going on, even just ask why he thought Warrick should get the "motorized conveyance," and then had settled for me. The fear worming its way through my bones overrode my curiosity, and I bolted from the room. One thing I did need was a coat before I did anything else.

I found one that wasn't too gross hanging on a hook by the door. This just kept getting weirder and weirder, but at least I now had a jacket.

I went back out into the cold. The zombie creature didn't even look at me. I hurried back to the room and knocked on the door.

Warrick opened it and pulled me inside. Harrison waited with him, looking even perkier than he had before. Warrick seemed fine, so I guessed the vampire was simply still recovering.

"We have to get the motorized conveyance from the stable area," I said.

"The what from the what?" Harrison scratched his head.

"I have no idea, but he gave me keys. Let's see if we can get out of here."

There were no other clothes in the room, so Warrick did a little magic to help me and him stay warm. Harrison told us the cold didn't really bother him. A very tiny part of me questioned if we were safe with Harrison, but so far, he hadn't done anything but thank us for our help. At this point, I felt better with him around.

We dashed out into the night. The wind whipped snow around us, gusting and creating little mini blizzards.

Harrison glanced around then pointed. "Parking lot? Motorized conveyance would be a car of some sort."

"Yeah, let's go."

The weather was kicking up again, and by the time we reached the parking lot the mini blizzards had turned into a real one. I wasn't sure if the snow was coming up from the ground, down from the sky, or both. It really didn't matter. No one should be driving in this.

But if it was a chance to get away, we had to take it, right?

There were a few semi-trucks in the parking lot and one large coach bus. I stared at the key in my hand and then the bus.

"Seriously?" *Fuck.*

"Any of you lot know how to drive that thing?" Harrison glanced back at us.

I snorted.

"How hard can it be?" Warrick took off for the bus at a jog.

I tried to follow at that pace and slipped on a patch of ice. Harrison's vampire-quick reflexes saved me from falling, and Warrick slowed.

"Sorry, love." My demon came back to my side.

"This is a terrible idea." I let Harrison help me across the icy parking lot until we reached the bus.

Warrick had the door open, and we all piled inside.

"Great. I'll drive," Warrick said, and put the key in the ignition, turning it.

Nothing.

The wind gusted, blowing the door open. It hadn't shut well behind us.

"Shut that," I snapped at Harrison.

"It doesn't latch!" the vampire pushed on the door again.

Warrick tried to start the bus again. And again there was no response, as if the battery was completely dead.

I racked my brain for an answer. "Um… I have no idea how I know this but there's a battery switch cut out."

"A what, luv?" Harrison tilted his head.

"A switch to make the battery work." I pushed past the vampire and hurried outside until I found a panel on the side of the coach toward the back. I worked the lever then ran back inside.

This time the lights flipped on when Warrick turned the switch. So did an awful squealing alarm.

We all winced but ignored it for now.

"Ahh, this I do know. It's a diesel, so you gotta wait a minute, Warrick." Harrison pointed to a coily symbol on the dash. It vanished. "Okay, try now."

Warrick turned the switch, and the bus gave an unearthly whine, shuddered, and failed to start.

"Ahh, fuck, mate. It's frozen. Too cold. Fuel or something."

Warrick swore and slapped his hand on the dash. A zing of energy even I could feel went through the bus, tingling at my feet and my hand where I leaned on a chair.

This time the engine caught, and the bus rumbled to life.

"Okay, great, so let's go. What is that horrible noise?"

"No idea," Warrick said. He pushed the button on the dash that had a "D" on it. The engine noise changed, but nothing happened when he pushed on the accelerator. Well, the engine revved, but the bus didn't move.

"What the fuck now?" I muttered. "We are so close."

Suddenly, the horrible screech stopped. We all jumped, looking around and wondering what the hell that was about.

The door finally shut seemingly on its own. Was the bus possessed?

"Ahh, parking brake." Warrick slammed his fist down on a yellow button, and the bus lurched forward. He'd left it in "D."

"There we go!" Warrick hit the accelerator hard, and the back end of the bus tried to come around and say hi to the front. It slammed into the side of a semi.

"Uh, maybe not so much on the ice." Harrison patted Warrick on the shoulder.

This time the bus cooperated, and Warrick drove toward what appeared to be a snow-covered road. As soon as we were out from between the semis, the bus rocked with a violent gust of wind.

"Yay!" I cheered.

Harrison gave me a cheeky grin. "So, where we going?"

"Away from here," Warrick said. "Hopefully we'll see a sign soon."

"Not going to see much of anything," I said as the snow swirled around us. I was desperate to be away, but maybe we should have waited?

"We'll just take it slow," Warrick said as he turned onto the snow-covered road. The bus rocked from another blast of wind. "It'll be fine."

Dakota Brown

CHAPTER 19

Mandy

"It'll be fine?" I glared at Warrick.

He stared back, wide-eyed. "I didn't know they could tip over."

"They're not supposed to!" I sighed dramatically and waved a hand around.

"To be fair, luv, I don't think they're designed for this kind of weather." Harrison, who wasn't nearly as bothered by the cold as Warrick or I, squeezed back into the cab of the now reclining coach bus, lowering himself until his feet hit the dash. He pulled the door shut over his head, but like before, it wouldn't seal. That was so weird. It only closed properly when the bus was running, apparently.

The draft of cold air that followed was far less welcome than the vampire.

Warrick's magic, fortunately back to nearly full function, was keeping us warm. That was something, anyway. And the influx of cold dissipated.

"You never say it'll be fine. Because then it's not fine. Unless you're saying it ironically, and then it's okay." Even to me that was a little incoherent, but whatever.

Warrick's brow wrinkled with confusion as he tried to come to terms with my words.

Harrison patted the incubus on the shoulder. "Don't worry about it. Just agree with the lovely lady, and let's figure out what we're going to do next."

I grunted in annoyance. "Since your powers are working, can you contact Sabian? Or sense him, or anything?"

Warrick shut his eyes and turned his focus inward.

While he was doing that, I attempted to not replay the accident over in my mind for the hundredth time. The gust of wind, the swerving as Warrick lost control, the crash of the bus going over on its side on the road. The swirling whiteness everywhere. I was sure we were on the road. Beyond that, I had no idea.

Harrison had saved me from a great deal of damage by wrapping himself around me and taking the brunt of the force the side of the bus would have otherwise inflicted on my skull and shoulder.

This particular bus didn't have seatbelts except for the driver. I was increasingly grateful the vampire was with us.

The very attractive, seemingly kind, vampire.

Knowing Warrick could sense the direction of my imagination, I tried to turn it away from my inappropriate thoughts, but it was difficult.

Warrick glanced at me, arching an eyebrow before he glanced at Harrison. A sly smile curled his lips and he shrugged, not acting put out by my traitorous libido.

Harrison either didn't notice the exchange or ignored it.

Which was good, because now I was blushing.

"There is still some sort of barrier, but it is not as solid now. I think they're coming."

"Oh, good. Can you keep us warm until they get here?" I wrapped my arms around myself.

He clambered over the seatback and wrapped his arms around me. I nestled into his demonic warmth and stood, trying not to shiver because then I had to admit I was afraid, not just cold.

"With this weather they might not be able to reach us." Warrick shook his head. "Okay, right, they have magic. Way more magic than I do. And if they didn't bring that mage of theirs along, I'll be surprised."

"Brennan? Yeah, he is kind of a badass."

"Mandy, they're all badasses."

I snorted. "Have to be, to save the world."

Warrick conceded my point.

"Do you think she brought Mal?"

Warrick chuckled, well familiar with my platonic crush on the vampire. "Probably."

I sighed happily, and my incubus tightened his arms around me.

"Uh, friends, I think we have a problem."

Our gazes both shot to Harrison. "What?" we said in unison.

"Company coming." He shuddered. "Not the saving-our-butts kind, either, if my senses are correct."

"Hell," I muttered and buried my face in Warrick's chest. "What do we do?"

"Hide." Harrison moved toward the back of the bus and gestured for us to join him.

I had no idea where we'd hide, but I was starting to remember that empty-eyed creature from some suppressed memory. I remembered something about being told we were bait. But that was it. We had to get away.

***

I blinked, peering through the steam that filled the air around me. It was hot, moist, and felt very good after all the cold.

What cold?

I frowned and focused more carefully. I sat in a hot tub. In my clothing. The wind was howling, and the ends of my hair were starting to freeze as the storm raged. I wasn't as hot as before. I was immersed in the water almost to my chin to stay warm.

Wait, before?

What was going on? Why was this familiar? I'd never even thought about getting in a hot tub fully clothed. That was a minimal clothing sort of activity. Even in a blizzard.

I was alone. Why was that weird?

Twisting around, I tried to figure out what was going on without getting frost bite. The wind whipped at me, and I sank down again. What was I going to do?

And how did I end up in this situation in the first place?

Where was Warrick? He was supposed to be here. Wasn't he?

The water was cooling, and I started to shiver. I was going to freeze to death in a hot tub in the middle of a blizzard. How was that even a thing?

There was a hotel? I vaguely remembered a hotel.

I fished in my pockets but couldn't find a key.

Damn it.

If I got out, I'd probably die if I couldn't get inside in minutes. If I didn't get out, I'd die, but maybe not quite as quickly.

Well, if I was going to go, I'd rather go doing something than waiting for it to happen. I managed to locate what I thought was the hotel through the swirling snow, though for the life of me I couldn't remember why I knew there was a hotel there.

Taking a deep breath and praying I wasn't making a mistake, I launched myself out of the hot tub and sprinted as fast as my rapidly freezing clothing, the snow drifts, and the blinding wind would let me. I had no sense of my surroundings. I could have been running across snow-covered pavement, or through a garden, for all I knew. My vision narrowed to my goal. Get to the hotel and get inside before I froze to death.

I made it to the shelter of the hotel, but my fingers wouldn't cooperate when I found a likely door to try to open. I slammed into it, the pain from hitting my frozen shoulder against the wood, pain breaking through the numbness from the cold.

I cried out.

The door opened, and I fell inside, the warm air almost painful.

"Who the fuck are you?" a feminine voice snapped.

My jaw was locked up. Scratch that, my entire body was locked up.

"Shannan, she's freezing. Let's ask questions later."

The next hour or two were a blur, but eventually I regained some semblance of consciousness and actual awareness sitting curled up on a hotel bed, buried in blankets, and clutching a steaming mug of soup.

Two women watched me from the uncomfortable looking, cracked vinyl chairs against the opposite wall.

"Ahh, there you are," one of the women said.

At some point I'd heard at least one of their names, but for the life of me I couldn't remember it. I was usually good at names. Right now, I could barely remember my own. Where was I? Why did I feel like I'd been asking that question for a while.

The two women looked similar, as if related, but not quite twins. Both had long reddish-brown hair, brown eyes, and pale skin. They were both dressed like lumberjacks. Heavy boots, jeans, turtlenecks, and red plaid flannels at least made me think of lumberjacks. I'd never actually met one, so I didn't know how they dressed.

"Thank you." I couldn't help the quaver in my voice, and I covered my uncertainty with a taste of the soup.

It wasn't anything special. Probably soup from a can and heated in a microwave. It tasted delicious at that moment, and before I knew it, the mug was empty. I wasn't wearing anything under the blanket. While that was a little distressing, I suspected I would have been more physically distressed if they'd left my clothing on me. Quite possibly dead.

"So, who are you, and why in the nine hells were you soaking wet and outside in this weather?" The one woman asked. She had something of a drawl. Texan? Probably.

"Uh. I don't know." I hunched my shoulders. I was still cold, but I wasn't shivering uncontrollably at least.

"You don't know?" the other woman said. "Honey, you on drugs?"

"Uh. No." I shivered at the thought. "At least, I didn't take any that I know of. If I was drugged, I don't remember. Uh, you don't have a phone, do you?"

"Tower's out. Reception and landlines are down. This storm is awful. We were lucky to get a room. We'll be lucky if our rig starts when this blows over. It's been like this for a week."

"Do you know where we are?"

Just as one of the women was about to answer, the door slammed open.

They squawked in alarm, and I startled.

"Oh, fuck!" My memories came slamming back into me, and I tried to scramble from the bed and entangling blankets. I had to run.

***

Steam swirled around me, and a heavy, wet warmth weighed on my shoulders, dragging me down.

164

I was sitting in a hot tub huddled in a blanket and everything was soaking wet.

"What the fuck?"

I'd been here before. Why was I in a blanket? Why was I naked? Tears leaked from my eyes.

The wind was calmer. Calmer than what?

Though the wet blanket was uncomfortable, it was warm with trapped heat, so I left it over my shoulders while I looked around.

Running hadn't worked.

I frowned, trying to remember, trying to get my fuzzy brain to focus. Why did it feel like I'd done this before?

I coughed, the tight feeling in my chest a new worry that I didn't have time to deal with.

"What's that?"

Someone's voice carried on the wind. A sharp, female voice I didn't recognize.

I didn't hear a response.

Did I run? And if so, away from or toward the voice?

The choice was taken from me as some white-parka-clad figures came into view through the mist and swirling snow.

"What the hell are you doing?" the sharp female voice demanded.

"Question of the night," I replied, teeth chattering while trying to stifle another cough.

"Stanton! Get the survival gear. We need to get her out of there!"

The next few minutes were a blur as these newcomers got me out of the water, into a heated vehicle, dry and clothed.

Once I was dry, the wracking coughs started along with the questions. Unfortunately, I didn't have any answers. They were also very cagey about who they were.

Exhaustion tugged at my eyelids, and I struggled to stay awake, certain my life depended on me remembering something, anything, from the last however long it had been since Warrick and I had been hiking in the desert.

Warrick! Where was he?

That was the last thought I had as oblivion claimed me.

CHAPTER 20

Price

Even with Brennan's magic, the driving conditions were heinous. Though Inferno didn't normally let me go anywhere without him, he'd managed to convey that he would only be a shout away. If we'd known where we were going, we could have tried to make a portal, but the spell was being blocked and we only had a general direction. Mandy and Warrick were north, so we went north up I25, and kept going. Colorado was almost behind us. We thought. It was getting hard to tell where we were at, and cell reception was almost nothing. We might already be in Wyoming for all we knew.

"This is nice," I muttered, my fingers buried in Mayhem's fluff while he sat on my lap. Mal with his vampire sight and reflexes was driving through the bubble of clear air Brennan had been creating for the last couple of hours.

"We can keep going," Brennan said, voice quiet not showing any sign of strain. I could feel his fatigue through the mark we shared, though.

"Brennan, let's take a break and do the tracking spell again," I suggested.

He shook his head. Mal found an exit anyway, taking my hint. He was probably feeling the strain, too.

I was antsy. The interstate was about as straight as it could be, so I didn't even have to navigate.

Mal left the vehicle running, and we parked by the side of the road while Brennan dropped the magic. He didn't hide the sigh of relief, which I counted as a win. He was becoming more comfortable with showing his emotions around us, and that was good.

The SUV, now exposed to the elements, rocked with the wind, and snow piled up on the windshield. Even though we were in a warm vehicle, I shivered.

Mal pulled out the paper map and quickly performed the spell. The pendulum swung north.

"If it's any consolation," Brennan started, "I'm pretty sure that means she's somewhere along the interstate. There's been no real deviation since we got on I25 in New Mexico."

"That's something." I crawled into the back of the SUV and gestured for Brennan to turn. When he put his back to me, I dug my fingers into his muscles until his shoulders eased as he took another deep breath.

"Thank you, Chris." He actually leaned back against me and let me wrap my arms around him.

I caught Mal's smile in the rearview mirror as I held the mage.

"It is not so difficult," Brennan said. "Just draining over the length of time we've been traveling. I can resume in a few minutes."

"Just tell us if you need a break. In this weather I can't imagine Mandy and Warrick are going very far."

"True." Brennan took another deep breath then sat back up. "We should continue if you're up for it, Mal."

"I'm doing all right." The vampire put his hands back on the wheel.

Brennan cast the spell, and we went back into the storm.

***

Ages later, we finally had to stop for the night. We'd been driving straight through for more hours than we cared to think about, and we were all tired. Not to mention, we were almost out of fuel and Brennan was just tired enough that he didn't trust himself to conjure more without rest unless it was an emergency. Chugwater, Wyoming had a hotel. It wasn't a good hotel, but Brennan assured me he had enough power left to cast a cleaning spell on the room if I couldn't manage it. Assuming there were any rooms left.

Mal found a parking spot and waited with the car while Brennan and I braved the storm, Mayhem tucked under my arm. The wind whipped around us, tugging at our clothing and making me wish I hadn't shaved the sides of my head. Still, we were inside faster than it was worth casting a spell to keep myself comfortable.

I wrinkled my nose at the haze of stale cigarette smoke that hung in the air. The walls were yellowed, and it wasn't clear what color they had once been. The vinyl on the furniture was cracked and the foam on the inside brown instead of yellow. I wanted to get hit with a power washer to clean off the ick just walking into the place.

Brennan must have caught my disgust through our bond because he shot me a quick grin before sparing me from having to touch anything by tapping the bell on the counter. The sign said ring for service.

We waited for an oddly long amount of time before a harried-looking woman hurried into view. She had graying hair up in curlers, though she looked relatively young. Her sack-like flower-print dress did nothing for her aesthetically but looked comfortable enough, and she had a cigarette in one hand.

"How in the hell did you two get here? Road's been closed for days." Her voice was rough from her smoking, and she squinted at us suspiciously.

"Carefully," Brennan deadpanned. "Do you have a room available?"

She glanced at the back room for a moment before shrugging and studied something behind the counter while she muttered under her breath.

"Got one. Hundred a night."

I raised my eyebrows. That was robbery for a place like this, but at this point I wasn't going to say anything. I dug out my wallet, pulled out a couple of fifties and exchanged it for a key. She didn't even ask for a credit card. That never happened anymore.

"How long is the storm supposed to last?" Something was bugging me about this entire thing. Unfortunately, I couldn't figure out what. Too long on the road maybe, and my brain was foggy.

"Don't know." She shrugged. "Need anything else?"

That was a clear dismissal. Brennan and I traded a quick glance before we turned and left the lobby. The cold air was a punch to the lungs, but at least it was clean. We hurried to the car and got in. Snow had already accumulated on the upwind side.

Mal turned on the wipers to get some of it off. "Anything?"

"She had one left." I showed him the key. It was a first-floor room in the strip of rooms near the office.

Mal moved the car, and we parked in front of the door.

"Ready for this?" I braced myself against the cold and thought about casting the spell that would protect me from the weather. I waited until the two men agreed, then opened the door and forced myself out into the cold. I couldn't help the shriek that tore from my mouth this time around. Mayhem disappeared in a swirl of snow. The wind stole the sound away as I slammed the door shut behind me and bolted for the room. I jammed the key into the lock with shaking hands and got the door open before frostbite set in. Brennan and Mal were right behind me with our things. Even Mal, who wasn't overly impacted by the weather, hunched his shoulders.

Brennan held up his hand, preparing to cast the spell when Mal went still in the way only a vampire could. "Wait," he said.

Brennan and I stared at Mal expectantly while he took a few steps farther into the room and inhaled deeply through his nose as if scenting the air. Mayhem copied his actions, sniffing around the room.

"Mandy and Warrick and one other were here."

The hellhound woofed seemingly in agreement.

"How long ago?" I studied the room as if I had a hope of sensing what the vampire had.

Brennan and I stayed just inside the door while Mal moved around the room, investigating. I could feel the cold radiate from the cracks around the door and jumped when the heater rattled to life next to me at the window. It was warmer in here than outside, though I wouldn't have exactly called it warm. The heater was trying.

"Not long. The room has been cleaned, but about as well as you might expect for a place like this, especially in the middle of a raging storm." Mal returned, a frown marring his brow. "I think the other person that was in here was a vampire. I'm not positive. I smell blood, but only a hint on the air as if blood were spilled but not violently."

"What do we do?"

Mal sighed. "We get some rest. Even I'm tired. I'd like to go charging out into the storm and find our friends, but at this point the only one who hasn't been doing magic or hyper focusing on anything for a while is you, and you are improving rapidly, but this weather will kill you if you make a mistake."

I grumbled. "Yeah, mate, I know I suck at the fine control shit."

Brennan laughed. "We all do, when we first start. Even fae."

"Oh." Between his words and his laughter, I felt a lot better. His comment meant a lot to me, especially paired with the emotion. He'd dared to laugh at me and that was precious.

"Okay, fine, so, we sleep." I crossed my arms under my breasts and wondered how in the hell I was going to manage that. I was tired but worry for Mandy and Warrick was higher on my list of concerns than sleep.

Mal's expression went from weary to something a bit more predatory, and a small smile curled the corner of his mouth.

I bit my lip, heart picking up a little.

Mal's gaze flicked from me to Brennan then back again.

"I will clean the room," Brennan said. "I have no objection to watching, if you two wish to wear each other out."

"No objection isn't the same as wanting to, or enjoying," I said. "Only if it's something you will enjoy."

"Ahh, I misspoke. I will enjoy watching you, and I will enjoy learning more about what you like." Brennan waved his hand, and I felt the magic wash over the room.

Mal still went so far as to yank the comforter off the bed, so we didn't have to wonder where it had been, even with Brennan's cleaning. Under the blankets, the sheets were crisp white linens, and that was much more pleasing.

My vampire fixed his predatory gaze on me. Involuntarily, I backed up, bumping into Brennan. He clamped his hands down on my arms, immobilizing me.

Mal rumbled in approval while I mock struggled.

"I understand the game, and I feel your desire. Feel free to struggle if that makes it more fun for you." Brennan's breath tickled my neck as he whispered in my ear.

"Oh, okay!" My voice was breathy as I jerked, trying to get away from the mage, but he had a solid grip. I hadn't expected it, and my heart jumped a little at the feeling of being trapped without being bound. I did have to make sure I didn't let my emotions go too far into realistic fear or my wards would kick in, but I wasn't afraid. These men would never hurt me, and it made me more than thrilled that Brennan was participating.

I knew what was coming. The skillful way Mal would tease me with a hint of pain and a lot of pleasure. My skin flushed and a needy heat settled deep inside me.

"Do you want her?" Mal asked, voice low, eyes not leaving me.

"I do," Brennan's grip on my arms tightened, shocking me further.

"Then tell me what you want to do to our little exorcist," Mal ordered.

"I want you to tie her to the bed and hold her down while I taste her, and once I've had my fill, I want you to make her scream for us." The quiet intensity in his voice matched the heat in Mal's eyes.

"Oh, fuck me," I murmured, legs going weak. My skin tingled with the thought of how these two men would wreck me. I knew why Brennan wanted me tied down, and I objected not at all. Brennan and I had done intimate things before, but this would be the furthest he'd gone to this point, and I was seriously excited he wanted to do this with us.

I wanted to keep up the prey pretense, but my legs were barely supporting me and instead of my normal fast protest and attempt at escape, I let out a needy moan and sagged into the mage. The firmness of his erection pressed into my back, arousing me even more.

Mal took me from Brennan and tossed me over his shoulder for the very short trip to the bed. He threw me onto it, quickly sitting on my hips in case I got ideas of running. Not that there was anywhere to go in the hotel room, but I would have tried normally. Instead, my head was swimming in anticipation of Brennan's attentions.

Unsurprisingly, the mage had also provided ropes for Mal to tie me down with.

"Chris, if anything bothers you or you're uncomfortable, tell us to stop and we will," Mal said, as he always did when he tied me. Even though I could effectively use magic to untie myself, we always went over the rules.

"I will."

"Good." Then he leaned over and yanked my shirt over my head. My bra went next, and if I hadn't been used to vampire speed, I would have been impressed with how quickly he secured my hands above my head. I didn't know what he tied them to, but I was bound tightly and wasn't going anywhere before he got off my hips to pull down my pants.

I gave a few good yanks, but everything was secure and there was no way I was getting free without magic. Good.

As soon as Mal had my pants off, I twisted, as if trying to cover my front and free myself. This gave them a great view of my ass. Mal smacked it, just hard enough to sting, before rubbing the hand mark gently. I yelped happily.

He then grabbed my leg with both hands and flipped me on my back, not letting go of my ankle and quickly and efficiently securing it so that my knee was bent, and my ankle was tied to my thigh. A pretty lattice of ropework threaded up my leg, and then he secured my ankle to my bed, so my legs were spread.

I completely approved.

Cool air breathed across my heated skin as the radiator kicked on again. The air tickled across the small hairs on my legs and my mound, cooling but not diminishing my heated arousal.

Once Mal had my other leg secured, I was trussed and on display for the mage. I glanced at Brennan and was treated to the rare sight of naked desire in his eyes.

"You may have as much of me as you want, Brennan," I said.

Mal, taking advantage of the magical nature of our ropes, dragged me by my hips down to the edge of the bed so my butt was not quite hanging off it. I was secure, not going anywhere.

Brennan nodded and came forward, kneeling on the ground between my legs.

I groaned in anticipation, eyes fluttering shut as Brennan touched me gently, and expertly, with his hands on the inside of my thighs. He ran them up my legs until he reached my folds.

"You're very wet, Chris," he murmured against my inner thigh.

"Just for you, Brennan." I hoped it wouldn't hit a trigger but needed to say something.

"Good," he whispered.

While Brennan was hesitant to engage normally, he was far from lacking skill. He gently ran a finger through my dampness before sliding it inside of me.

I pushed against his hand, desperately wanting more.

"Behave," Mal ordered. "Let him have control."

"Sorry." I tried to relax while hearing Brennan laugh quietly.

The mage curled his finger, quickly finding my G spot and just as quickly finding my clit with his lips.

Words failed me, reducing me to incoherent groans as he tasted me with his lips, sucking and licking, while curling his finger inside of me. He used a touch of magic to stimulate me, along with his skilled mouth and fingers and he had me screaming out his name as I twisted against the bonds, wanting—no, needing more. I needed the release he was dragging me toward, and he was drawing it out. I knew he was. I was so close to the edge, and it was taking everything I had not to throw myself against him.

Brennan knew I had no patience, especially when it came to orgasms, and he was deliberately torturing me. I wanted to laugh in delight and scream in frustration. Instead, I concentrated on enjoying this moment he was giving me.

Finally, when I didn't think I could take it any longer, Brennan had mercy on me. Whatever he'd done to block me from coming sooner, he stopped, and my orgasm rippled through me in an intense storm that rivaled the one outside. It was made all the sweeter by it having been Brennan who brought me there.

I arched up on the bed, shouting in relief as my body fractured and reformed, especially when Brennan continued to lick my juices as I came.

He rumbled in satisfaction as my body finally quieted. Sweat drenched my skin, and I lay there, feeling wrung out.

"That was excellent," I managed to get out.

Brennan squeezed my ankle before stepping back.

He and Mal exchanged a few words I didn't catch before the vampire replaced Brennan between my legs. He was naked and more than ready to pick up where the mage had left off.

I met Mal's eyes and raised an eyebrow. His quick smile and nod let me know everything was okay with our mage, and I turned my focus onto the vampire.

"You need blood?"

"I do. And you need more orgasms."

I chuckled. "Do your worst."

Mal laughed, the sound low and predatory, going straight to my core. "Brennan wants you screaming, and so do I."

"What will the neighbor's think?" I acted scandalized.

Mal licked his lips. "Why would I care?" And with that he took his cock in his hands and guided the head to my entrance.

"But..." I mock protested.

"Scream, exorcist," he ordered and slammed himself into me.

By the time Mal was done with me, I was sure we'd woken the entire hotel. Brennan had returned for another round of bringing me screaming to climax, and I was completely exhausted. Sleeping would not be an issue tonight.

CHAPTER 21

Price

Waking cuddled between two of my guys was my favorite way to return to consciousness, even if I was in the middle of nowhere Wyoming in an unnaturally intense blizzard. At least I was warm.

I lay sprawled half over Mal's chest, and Brennan was curled up behind me, spooning with me. Mayhem was on the pillow next to my head. Brennan kissed my shoulder when I stirred.

"Morning," I mumbled.

"Morning, Chris," he replied sleepily.

Mal stroked my arm.

"We should get up. Mandy needs us," I said without moving. I wasn't quite awake enough to put motion behind my words. I did urgently feel that she needed us, but the languid relaxation in my limbs was hindering my motivation.

"I feel recovered," Brennan said, running his hand over my back.

The two of them were not helping my motivation, but we all knew Mandy needed us. I could feel their agreement through the bonds our marks formed between us.

"Okay, so we will recreate this cuddle experience soon, but I'm getting up because I'm human and have a human bladder." I grumbled. "Also, I really am worried about Mandy."

"We are too," Brennan agreed.

I worked my way out from between my two men and headed to the bathroom. We took turns cleaning up in the small space and getting ready for the day. Brennan even summoned some food for us.

Our cell reception had returned at some point, though we couldn't get calls to go out, so I sent a few messages off to the group text letting everyone know our status. Thanks to our marks, everyone knew we were okay.

Well, almost everyone. Lucifer and I had not renewed our marks after they'd been lost when he'd essentially been killed. I felt the ache keenly and rubbed at the blank circle in my ink where his elaborate demon mark had once been. I wanted it back, but we hadn't really addressed that yet. We were still feeling our way in the relationship, though he had come back to me. I resolved to bring it up with him after Mandy was safe. I'd been moving at his pace, but I had wants, too.

Mal touched the small of my back before leaning over and kissing me. "As soon as you're done, we'll repeat our tracking spell."

I stuffed the last of my food in my mouth and gave him a thumbs up.

Mal smiled and reached for the map he was using when a knock at the door interrupted us. My vampire froze before inhaling deeply, scenting the air. His eyes widened and he glanced at Brennan. The mage held up his hands, ready to cast and Mal went to the door. Mayhem growled softly.

I'd seen zombies before. Sort of. People who had their souls ripped out by demonic forces. It was every bit as scary as it sounded. This was somehow worse. The creature's skin was stretched over its skull. Its hair was thin and lank, and its eyes jaundiced. Its body looked like a human skin had been stretched over bones and not stuffed with any organs. The clothing it wore did nothing to disguise the skeletal nature of the creature.

It was probably a zombie. A fucking terrifying one. Hopefully it was the slow sort, not the supernaturally fast type that could run down a human for their brains. This guy needed more than brains though. He needed the whole set of organs.

"Come, the master will see you." It turned and walked away as if expecting us to follow.

"Uhhhhh—" I glanced at Brennan. "The fuck is that?"

The mage had paled. "Zombie. Different than the ones created for the attempted apocalypse."

"Should we follow?" I clenched my jaw and reached for my well of power. It responded, so there was that. I had no idea what was going on with my magic recently, but I was starting to have a thought, at least about why my portals were unstable. I touched the bare spot on my chest where an elaborate demon mark should be. I needed to talk to Lucifer.

"Sure," Mal replied uneasily.

I bundled up as much as I was able, cast a little environmental magic, and followed Mal and Brennan out into the storm, Mayhem on my heels.

The zombie led us back toward the main building, into the smoke-yellowed lobby and back into a meeting room.

Inside, in a parody of a mafia drama, a man sat behind a cheap conference room table in a wheeled chair. He faced away from us, and slowly spun around when we entered.

At his feet, bound and gagged, was Warrick. Other beings were in the room. I didn't pay a lot of attention to them. Brennan and Mal scanned the rest of the room for me.

The man in the chair pinged all my senses. He had dusky olive skin, prominent cheek bones, and dark wavy hair. The only way I could think of describing him was gaunt, as if he'd been starved for years and only recently gotten even close to enough to eat.

Yeah, this was likely our crazy vampire. Or whatever he was.

Growling, Mayhem shifted into hellhound form.

His expression was vacant as he scanned the room, and that was creepy enough. Clearly some thought was brewing in his head, but it wasn't obvious what. Then, when his attention landed on Mal, his eyes and attention focused.

I'd faced down some of the most powerful entities in Heaven and Hell, and right then I'd have taken Mammon's return over the look this guy leveled on Mal.

Part of it was the sheer avarice, the desire naked in his eyes. He wanted to possess my vampire. The other part of it was the absolute inhuman malice. I'd seen some scary shit, but that being's focused gaze was the worst yet.

Maybe it was simply because I didn't know how to fight it.

Well, one thing almost always worked. I pulled on my well of demonic energy gifted to me by Lucifer and gathered it into a ball.

This drew the creature's gaze to me, but I didn't care. It was easier to deal with evil when it was directed at me instead of someone I loved.

"You've got something of mine, asshole," I said.

He tilted his head as if considering my words before he rose to his feet and stalked toward me.

"Chris," Mal hissed urgently. He reached for me but I avoided his grasp.

"Get Warrick," I snapped, keeping my attention on the creature. Through our bond, I could feel Brennan also gathering energy for a spell. Mayhem positioned himself in front of me, hellfire lighting up his eyes.

The creature shifted his attention to my mage and smiled, showing grotesquely elongated fangs and blackened, pointed teeth. If he was a vampire, he certainly wasn't the same kind I was used to.

I threw my hands forward, palms toward the creature. A gout of hellfire erupted from my outstretched hands and blasted into the vampire-thing.

His scream curdled my blood and pounded against my eardrums.

Brennan, instead of attacking the creature directly, grabbed Warrick with magic and yanked him back toward us.

I clapped my hands over my ears.

Mal grabbed my arm and Warrick's, dragging the incubus and me out of the room before the creature could recover. Brennan was right behind us. Mayhem scrambled along with me, and I got a sense through my bond with Inferno that he was moments away from bursting into the hotel. I told him to hold off and that I'd shout if we needed him.

My mage slammed the door shut and threw up a shield. Mal let go of my arm. I was definitely going to have bruises, but my wards had recognized my vampire and not thrown him off me. Fortunately.

Mal tugged the bonds off Warrick and roughly removed the gag. "Where's Mandy?"

The incubus blinked and shook his head, as if trying to shake off something.

"Warrick, where is she!" Mal shouted.

Warrick's mouth moved without anything coming out.

"Mal, the creature may have some sort of control over Warrick. We have to move." Brennan tugged on Mal's arm, urgently.

My vampire swore and threw Warrick over his shoulders in a fireman's carry. Damn my vampire was strong.

A crash against the door we'd just come through and the reek of burned meat distracted me from my appreciation. We scrambled for the exit just in time to nearly plow over a very familiar-looking woman. She was wrapped in a mottled white and gray parka and snow pants, but the stormy gray eyes and perpetual frown on the lean, angular face were very familiar. A couple other men were with her, and they already had weapons pointed our direction.

I charged forward as Yashira, the inquisitor bitch I'd met in Thailand, pressed the trigger on her gun. Not flinching as the muzzle flashed and the bullet sped right toward me was nearly as hard as staring down the creature in the other room.

My wards activated, shattering the bullet, just as another loud crack signaled the arrival of the creature breaking through the door. Mayhem's roar assured me he was holding off the creature for a few moments.

Yashira hadn't expected me to be able to take a direct hit and keep on coming. She folded with an *oof* as my shoulder drove into her stomach. The gun went off again, deafening me, but my wards protected me, and everyone behind me. I took the inquisitor to the ground, then I was behind her. Brennan and Mal joined me. Warrick hung limply over Mal's shoulders.

The inquisitor scrambled to her feet, but the creature's enraged roar distracted her from us. She turned, bringing her gun up and firing. My hearing was already shot, the sound muffled, but I did hear Mayhem yelp. Wait? Was she still hunting us? I was going to kill that bitch if she hurt my dog. Fortunately, Mayhem bounded through her men before she could do more than piss him off. He belched another gout of hellfire toward the inquisitors and caught one of the men, but not Yashira.

I glanced at my guys. Mal scented the air, his eyes narrowed as he zeroed in on Yashira.

Interesting. I couldn't hear a damn thing, so I didn't ask him what was up. Through our bond, I felt resolve replace a moment of shock. We sprinted outside, leaving the inquisitors to deal with whatever we'd left behind. If, in fact, they were here to deal with the creature, and weren't working with him.

Mal dragged me close once we were outside and shouted in my ear, though it still came across muffled. His words chilled me more than the worst Wyoming blizzard.

"They have Mandy!"

CHAPTER 22

Price

The inquisitors had Mandy? If they'd hurt her, they would pay.

Mal, wisely, led us to our SUV. The wind whipped stinging snow in our faces and tugged at our bodies, trying to trip us up. Once we were inside, he didn't even try to get us out of there. We were probably at least partially protected by the storm unless they had some way to sense us. The SUV was covered in snow and even though we'd disturbed some, I imagined it would be coated again in short order.

My vampire had his map and pendulum out whispering the words to the tracking spell. Brennan had Warrick in the back and was casting gentle spells at the incubus.

"This way!" Mal leaped out of the car again. "She's close!"

"Brennan, keep an eye on Warrick, and be prepared to come get us." Mayhem and I dashed after my vampire.

I was lost in minutes in the swirl of the snow. Mal stayed with me. He and Mayhem both seemed to have caught Mandy's scent, or whatever it was Mal used to track people when he wasn't using magic.

The snow lent a timeless quality to the atmosphere. The drifts we had to blast our way through with magic, just made this entire thing more unreal. Some of them were taller than I was. Still, Mal and Mayhem led us on at a swift pace, and before long we were crouched down by a cement outbuilding that might have had something to do with utilities, but it was impossible to tell. About a hundred yards away, I could just make out a construction trailer through the snow.

"She's in there?"

My hearing had recovered, and I'd had to adjust my magic to filter out some of the insane howl from the wind.

Mal nodded.

"Anyone else?"

Mal glanced at me. His eyes had gone completely black as they did when he used his powers. "Yeah. Two others beside her. Mandy's temperature isn't right. She might be sick or injured."

There was time for questions later as to how Mal knew that. I reflected again that I didn't know a ton about vampires and should find out more. Someday. When we weren't in the middle of a crisis.

"What's the plan?" I asked.

"We're going to sneak up on the place. I'm going to go in and get her out, and then we're going to either get back to Brennan or portal somewhere safe."

"Good plan."

Mayhem whined, put his paw on Mal's arm then shook in disgust.

"New plan," Mal said. "You go in and get her out. Mayhem and I will wait outside as close as we can get."

I tilted my head.

"I think Mayhem means they've got some sort of ward up that would affect him and me. I can't sense it, but that's not out of the question."

"Think they have some sort of faith-based power that actually works?" Most didn't, in my experience.

The vampire nodded.

"Great, well, I have wards, too. Let's get her and get out of here." The drain of having to fight the blizzard was not large, but it was constant, and annoying.

Mal squeezed my shoulder, then we all moved forward as quickly as we could without being too obvious about it. We weren't camouflaged against the snow, but it would certainly hide us unless people were really paying attention.

We made it to the stairway up to the door of the trailer before Mal nodded. "Yeah, Mayhem and I would cause a stir if we went any farther. All yours, Chris." He grinned at me. "Give 'em hell."

"They'd better hope they haven't hurt her. Text Brennan and let him know?"

Mal nodded, and I started up the stairs. My skin tingled as I passed through what was probably their version of wards. It didn't stop me, though, and I suspected I didn't alert like a demon would. Well, if I had time to ask, I would, because it was possible I did. That might have bothered me at one point. Not now.

I paused by the door and listened. I couldn't hear anything over the storm anyway, so I figured charging in was my best option.

Reaching up, I grabbed the doorknob, twisted and shoved with as much strength as I could manage because I expected it to be hard to open. Instead, I went flying into the room and tripped, landing on my ass, which did give the bullets a chance to go sailing over my head instead of slamming into my wards.

I'd been prepared for everything but the falling on my ass bit, so I slammed the shooter with a wave of energy, tossing him backward over a chair. The other person must have been their mage. She chanted something vaguely familiar sounding. I threw up an extra shield, located Mandy, and scrambled over to her.

189

She looked like shit. Her skin was yellowed, sweat gleamed on her forehead, and the look she gave me was half delirious with fever.

Giving myself a magical boost, I gathered Mandy up into my arms and ran for the door. It slammed shut as I reached it.

"Fucking hell, you will," I snarled and shoved.

Too hard. Half the wall went with the door, exposing the inside to the elements, but that was not my problem.

I stumbled down the stairs. Mal caught us at the bottom. He took Mandy from me, looked at her, then back at me. "Portal us out of here," he ordered.

I really tried to take us back to the house, but portals made me think of Lucifer, and the portal magic was more than happy to dump us into Lucifer's throne room, where a demonic cheer went up when they saw me. Because of course there were a whole bunch of demons present.

"Mal?"

"I've got Mandy," he said.

I glanced and noticed him biting into his wrist. She must really be in bad shape if he was healing her with blood.

The assembled horde wasn't attacking, fortunately. A few of them were bowing low. Others just acted demonically happy to see me. Which was unsettling.

"My dear, whatever are you doing here?" Lucifer's voice reached me, and I spun around.

He gave me that panty-melting smile of his that I couldn't help returning. "Uh, portal malfunction."

"Ahh, I see." He rose from his throne and came over to me, eyes never leaving mine. "My demons love you. It's causing an emotional storm down here in Hell. That battle you had with them... Let's just say they think it was epic." Lucifer cupped my jaw with his hand before giving me a relatively chaste kiss on the lips.

Bruce, his hellhound, was at his side, and he and Mayhem exchanged friendly tail wags.

Lucifer turned his attention to Mal, who still sat on the ground, cradling Mandy in his arms. Her color had improved, but she was unconscious.

"What happened?" He swiftly kneeled, putting a hand on her forehead before standing and returning his attention to me.

"Not completely sure," I admitted. "She went missing. We tracked her down. We also might have found the vampire, creature, thing that escaped and has apparently been causing havoc on the surface."

"Ahh. Did you kill it?"

"No, but the hellfire sure pissed it off. Not sure if the inquisitors were working for or against, though. Maybe just take a look?"

With my permission, Lucifer delved into my recent memories, so I didn't have to update him completely.

"One moment." He formed a portal and stepped through. A few moments later, he returned with Brennan and Warrick.

The incubus looked much more aware of his surroundings and scrambled to Mal's side when he saw Mandy.

Lucifer vanished through the portal again. This time when he came back, a frown creased his forehead.

"Gone?" I guessed.

"The creature and the inquisitors have vanished."

"Never thought I'd be relieved to be in Hell," Brennan said. I gave him a quick hug before turning back toward Mandy.

She stirred in Warrick's arms.

"Should we get her out of here before she wakes up?"

Lucifer shrugged. "It may be best. I'll return you to your home."

191

"Thanks. Hey, uh, we need to talk. Soon." I sauntered over to him, grabbed the front of his shirt and dragged him down for a much less chaste kiss, which got at least some of the demons cheering.

"What about?"

I tapped the middle of my chest where his mark should have been.

"Ahh. Let me get you all home."

The trip home took moments, and my devil gave me another quick kiss. "Come back soon." And then he was gone.

I took that to mean he was willing to discuss. In the meantime, I turned all my attention to Mandy.

Warrick cradled her like a baby, and when her eyes finally fluttered open, she gazed at him with open love in her expression.

It took her a few minutes to really come to her senses though, and by then we had her installed on the couch. It was the middle of the afternoon, and no one was home, but my phone lit up shortly after Mandy started looking around the room, confused.

"Hi, Sabian, yes, we're home. Yes, we have Mandy and Warrick. Everything okay?"

"Yes, boss," he replied more business-like than normal, but nothing that alarmed me. Especially since his sense through our bond was content.

"Great. I'll see you soon."

"I'm looking forward to it." There was the dripping-sex voice.

"What happened?" Mandy asked once I'd hung up.

"We were going to ask you." Mal still kneeled next to her.

She looked at Warrick. "We woke up in the hot tub. And then, I was in the hot tub again. Harrison!" She bolted upright. "Where is he?"

Warrick's eyes widened. "I don't know. I don't remember much from when the bus crashed until Brennan woke me up."

"The bus crash?" I couldn't help but repeat.

"Uh." Warrick frowned. "Yeah. We tried to escape in a bus."

"Mal? Food?" I gave my mate a desperate glance.

He nodded and headed for the kitchen while Mandy and Warrick pieced together some of what had happened to them. Their tale was relatively incredible. Not that I didn't believe them, but it ended with them both desperate to find Harrison.

"Mal saved me again, didn't he?" Mandy asked after we'd eaten.

"Yeah, he did," I agreed. "You were in really bad shape." I didn't tell her he'd given her some of his blood. She could figure that out on her own.

She looked at Mal while he and Brennan cleaned up in the kitchen.

"Thank you."

Mal glanced in her direction and smiled before going back to work.

She shook her head. "I don't know what I'd do without all of you."

I gave Mandy a quick hug. "You're part of the extended Price family. We take care of our own. Now, why don't you get some rest, and then we'll see what we can do about this Harrison friend of yours."

"Thanks, Chris."

The hearty meal caught up with her, and her eyes fluttered shut as soon as she sat back down on the couch. Warrick helped her lay on her side and covered her with a blanket before giving me the biggest puppy-dog eyes ever.

"I don't know what I'd do without her. I couldn't keep her safe." His expression fell.

"Warrick," I patted his shoulder. "That monster is a scary freaking dude. You did the best you could. We'll have to stop it, and it'll probably take all of us to do it."

He took a deep breath and nodded. "Okay." His attention returned to Mandy.

I glanced at my guys in the kitchen. They were both staring at me, and not in a lustful way. Yeah, we needed to figure out what to do about this creature, and fast. If we were going to have a hard time standing against it, your run of the mill human was doomed.

Our silent communication was interrupted by a knock at the door. Surprised, since we hadn't been expecting anyone, I went and answered it.

"Darius! What do you want?" I crossed my arms and stared at my priest friend. He was the one who had gotten me into most of this in the first place, and by most, I do mean most, from the exorcist gig all the way up to being buried in a pile of men. It wasn't all bad, but he almost never showed up unless there was trouble involved.

Even more telling was when Gabriel stepped up next to him.

"Chris Price. The Vatican needs your help."

CHAPTER 23

Price

I burst out laughing. "Say again, mate?"

Gabriel just gave me a look.

"You'd better come in." I shut the door behind them.

Gabriel rested their fingers on Mandy's forehead when I followed them into the living room. Darius exchanged uneasy glances with the others before settling into Aaron's favorite chair.

"She will recover. The vampire's assistance was timely." They turned and perched on the edge of the loveseat.

"Would you like anything to drink?" Mal offered the room.

Gabriel shook their head as Darius accepted.

"Chris Price, would you summon the Adversary. We must discuss."

Darius went ashen and nearly choked on whatever it was Mal had given him to drink. Gabriel ignored the priest. I did, too.

"Yeah, sure. Give me a minute." It would have been really damn convenient if I could have just thought at him, but no, no more marks. Instead, I had to get up, run down into the basement, pop through the portal to Ezra's domain, and…

"Hi, Ezra!"

"Chris!" He turned and held out his arms.

I could not resist throwing myself against him. Especially since he was only about half dressed. He could, and often did, use magic to change his clothing. This time he'd apparently been doing it the human way, and I caught him mid-change, as the portal into his domain entered into his bedroom.

The hellhounds that guarded the entrance on this side might have alerted him, but he was happy to see me. The warm emotion flowed through our bonds and wrapped me up on the inside while he held me tight to his chest.

"You act like you are in a hurry. Otherwise, I'd detain you for a while," he said, voice lowering suggestively.

"Ugh, Gabriel is making me summon 'The Adversary.'" I mock groaned dramatically, though I couldn't resist reaching up and running my fingers along the soft ridges of his curled horns.

Ezra's eyes shuttered, and he rumbled softly in pleasure. Reluctantly, I pulled my hand away.

He smoothed my hair back and kissed my forehead. "Why?" Voice only a little husky from lust.

"I don't know. Something about the Vatican needing us, and probably something to do with the scary-ass vampire-creature thing that we set loose."

"I will join you." He released me before flipping his hand and then he was clothed in a deep green dress shirt and black slacks. We were going to see his boss, after all. Also, he knew how much I liked the slightly dressy look. He dressed more for me than he did for Lucifer, these days.

I took Ezra's hand and made another portal. It let us out into Lucifer's throne room. The room was still full of demons, and again they cheered when I entered. It hadn't been long since we'd been here previously, and Lucifer was still on the dais.

"Chris, is something wrong?"

196

"You'd fucking know if we still had our marks." I touched my chest, annoyed. I hadn't meant to say that, or even sound annoyed about it. Unfortunately, it slipped out.

"You are correct." He stood and came over to us. His tone told me nothing about how he felt about the situation.

I allowed him to pull me away from Ezra for another soul-stealing kiss before answering his question. Once I mentioned Gabriel, Lucifer rolled his eyes but nodded acceptance. "Let's go, then."

We portaled back into my living room. Technically, except for the portal in my basement, no one except me could make a portal into my house. Lucifer clearly had worked a loophole into my wards when he, Brennan, Mal, and Ezra had reinforced the house. Not that I was surprised.

Darius went even more ashen but nodded respectfully at Lucifer's greeting. I knew the devil had singled him out specifically because it made Darius squirm. I didn't add my own amused smirk to the mix, but it took some effort.

Sabian and Aaron had joined us by the time we got back, and Mandy was awake and sipping coffee while Warrick fussed over her like a mother hen. Lucifer found a spot on the loveseat.

"Chris Price, please tell us of what you know," Gabriel ordered.

I gave a quick recounting of what I knew of the last few weeks, including the encounter with the hunters and the inquisition. Mandy and Warrick filled in what they knew, and I watched Gabriel's child-like face grow more and more troubled.

"Adversary, do you recall dealing with this creature before?" Gabriel turned their attention to my devil.

"I do not believe I was the one that dealt with it before," Lucifer answered.

"Very well. We have lost the ability to contact anyone in the Vatican. Someone was able to get word to Father Darius, and he summoned us." Gabriel glanced over at Darius.

"You can't contact anyone?" Lucifer frowned. "That is troubling."

The archangel nodded. "To our vision, the day-to-day tourism continues. We have a proposal." Their attention shifted to Mandy, whose eyes widened.

"Yes?" She squirmed.

"You are known to the creature, yes, but we can disguise you. You will report what you see and return." Gabriel said this as if it were just a stroll in the park on Sunday.

"The fuck she will," I protested. "Disguise me. I'll do it."

"Your demons make this difficult," was the archangel's reply.

I glanced at Lucifer, and he shrugged. "Politics, I suppose."

"Mandy—"

"I'll do it," Mandy said. "But only because I want to rescue Harrison, too. I don't know what good I will do, however. I don't remember much from when the creature had me."

"Your memories will be restored." Gabriel stood and held out their hand.

"She's not recovered from her last encounter," I protested, shooting to my feet and standing in front of my employee.

"She is recovered," Gabriel replied. "In addition to her reconnaissance, Chris Price, you and the Adversary, and Aaron, and your mage, Brennan, will wait in the Vatican. It is not safe for any of your other men. Once Mandy has the information we require, we will refine our plan."

I wanted to object further. I really did. But I couldn't figure out how. Which is how I found myself kissing Ezra, Mal, and Sabian goodbye and stepping through an angelic portal for the first, or possibly second time if you counted when the angels had snatched me out of Hell a few months ago. It burned, and that tweaked me out a little. Specifically, it burned in the middle of my back where Ezra's mark graced my skin. Still, I'd accepted the demons into my life, and there were some consequences I couldn't avoid.

CHAPTER 24

Mandy

Kissing Warrick goodbye when I knew I was going into danger was so hard. He whispered, "Save Harrison if you can. Get him to join us if you want."

"Oh?"

Warrick winked. "I want him. You want him. Win-win."

My eyes widened. "Okay. I'll do what I can."

"He wants you, too."

The incubus would know, and I had no reason to argue. I hadn't set out to form my own group of men like Chris had. I was happy with Warrick, but I wasn't going to complain about adding a vampire into the mix if he was willing.

Then I joined Chris and the others and stepped through the portal. My heart was pounding, and I almost thought I might pass out from fear. How did Chris do it? I mean, now she had powers, but even before she only did exorcisms and simple spells, she still willingly went into danger.

Chris gave me an uneasy look on the other side of the portal. "You don't have to do this, Mandy. We can figure out another way."

"I should be relatively safe, right?"

Chris pursed her lips and didn't reply for a moment. "No. Probably not safe at all."

I sighed. "Okay, well, I'll just do my best."

Gabriel led us to a hotel and straight to a room. I had no idea how they had accomplished all this, but I didn't have time to question them. Once we were in the common area of the suite, the angel came over to me where I stood by the couch, reached up, and put their hand on my forehead.

Memories flooded back, slamming into me and dropping me on my ass in the common area. The creepy vacant expression on the thing's face. The even worse feeling when those eyes focused on me showing the absolute madness and lack of anything even remotely human. The terrifyingly long fangs...

I shuddered. I remembered the way the creature had bitten Harrison and Warrick and how they'd gone into the same vacant-eyed stare. The creature had told me he was creating an army to take over the world and that I was bait. Then he'd delved into my mind, and I'd ended up in the hot tub again. For some reason, I was able to resist better than others and I'd woken up.

"Ick. I feel like I need a shower." I rubbed my arms and shook my hands.

Gabriel touched my forehead again and the feeling eased.

"Thanks."

They nodded. "You know what to watch for now. Go in. Observe. Return to us quickly."

I wasn't so sure I was glad I had those memories back, but all the same, it was done.

Chris put her hand out, stopping me from leaving. "She won't be recognized? And what if they are speaking a language she doesn't know?"

Gabriel tilted their head, considering. "A fair point, Chris Price." The angel turned to me. "I will give you the gift of Babel, and a temporary disguise."

"Wait, what!" I exclaimed as the angel again touched my forehead. I didn't feel any different when they took their hand away, but I was certain they'd done something.

"Now, return quickly." Gabriel gestured toward the door.

This time, Chris moved out of my way but the deep furrows on her brow let me know how unhappy she was about this.

"What did they mean, gift of Babel?" I whispered when I walked past her.

That got a slightly evil grin to curl her lips. "Think you might have a future as a translator, mate. If you want to leave the pizza shop."

"Right," I muttered as I left the room. I reminded myself that I had to find Harrison, took a deep breath, and headed out into the humid afternoon. This was a vast improvement from the blizzard, so I wasn't going to complain about the weather.

It took me a few minutes to notice that I understood everything everyone was saying. It wasn't like the words translated in my head. No. I actually understood the language being spoken.

"Whoa, trippy," I said to myself as I walked toward the gates into the Vatican. The line wasn't long, and in a few minutes, I was walking into the walled city, gawking just like any other tourist. People thronged around me, jostling me and looking as wide-eyed as I felt.

At first, everything seemed normal. Well, as much as I could tell from not having ever been here before. Something caught my attention about the ordained folk moving around the courtyards. There was a stiffness to their motions. Maybe?

Trying to calm my racing heart, I headed over toward a statue as if I were interested in it and made my way closer to one of the priests, or whatever rank he was. He stood there, unnaturally still like he was guarding the statue or something.

When I got close, I studied the marble figure and watched the priest out of the corner of my eye. That vacant stare was very familiar.

"Excuse me," I said, hoping it came out in Italian.

The priest slowly turned his head to look at me. "I'm closed," he replied before turning his head away. He didn't move the rest of his body.

I couldn't help scooting away as quickly as possible.

"Holy hell," I muttered. Not that I wanted to repeat that experience, ever, but I tried again with two other priests with the same results. I was afraid of attracting attention, so I went back to observation.

I was staring at a giant brass ball trying to figure out what to do next when a nun approached me.

She made the sign of the cross, put her hands together in a prayerful pose, and made a slight bow.

"You have the mark of Gabriel about you," she said in Italian.

Not only could I understand the languages, but I knew what language they were speaking just by listening. I was going to marvel at this later. Right now the mission was cramping my enjoyment a bit.

"Sister," I said quietly, not looking directly at her and hoping that was the correct form of address.

"We need help." Her voice quavered, but I sensed a great deal of strength under her fear.

"We're aware," I answered.

"Follow me."

Against my better judgement, I followed the nun. This was either a terrible idea, or she would have vital information for us. Or that was what I told myself, anyway. We swiftly left the main courtyard area and went into a side building.

Expecting a trap at any moment, I nearly leaped out of my skin when the door shut behind us. Nothing happened and the nun gave me a sympathetic look.

"We believe we are safe here. A few of our sisters have been consumed, but the majority of us were able to resist the creature."

Not quite reassured, I still nodded and followed her through the building. If it had been any other time, I would have been marveling at the beautiful but austere surroundings. As it was, I focused on the woman I followed. The air was still and peaceful and our footsteps clicked on the marble floor.

She led me into a side room where several other nuns and two men were seated around a large, round table. They all glanced up at our entrance. The room was full of books, plush furniture that looked like it might be as old as Mal, and as well preserved, and an unlit fireplace took up a large chunk of one wall.

"She has the mark of Gabriel, Your Holiness," the nun who had found me said at the man's questioning gaze.

He wore some sort of elaborate set of robes and looked like he must be important.

A vaguely familiar woman stood. She had short blond hair, wore a white suit, and had stormy gray eyes. She rested both hands on the table and leaned forward, glaring at me.

"You are with the demons. They, and the exorcist took you from us in Wyoming."

"Uh, well, I guess." I shrugged. No sense in denying it. I guess whatever Gabriel had done to disguise me had worn off. Or it didn't work on the holy folks.

The man's gaze turned stony, and the nun who had retrieved me took a step back, crossing herself again.

"Gabriel brought us here. They said you needed help, and clearly, they were correct." The last came out defensively, but I couldn't help myself.

"She has the mark of the angel," the nun repeated. "I am certain of it."

His Holiness—Did that mean he was the pope?— waved the woman in the suit back. "This entire situation was caused by the exorcist and her demons."

"It was not!" I took a step forward, fists clenched. "Michael was being a dick and trying to start the apocalypse. Chris was just trying to protect people she cared about and save the world. What were you doing? Working for Michael? He was trying to end the world. Well, screw you." I spun and headed for the doors. If they didn't want our help and just wanted to lay blame, then I was done. Perhaps I was channeling a bit of my boss. Maybe I had just hit the end of my tolerance. Either way, I was done. I would go tell Gabriel what I'd seen and then try to rescue Harrison, or probably more accurately, get Chris to help me. I'd been inside these walls long enough.

"Wait!" The pope commanded. He had to be the pope.

I ignored them, stomping toward the door.

"Messenger, my pardon. Please wait."

The politeness in his tone finally got me to stop and turn back around.

"How is it that you speak Italian so fluently? You do not even have an accent as most Americans would."

"That's what you care about? Unbelievable." Yeah, I'd definitely been hanging out with my boss too much. "Gabriel gave me the gift of Babel so I could do reconnaissance and come back and report to them."

This caused a bit of a stir, and even the woman in the suit acted surprised.

"What is your message?"

"I was to come in, look around, and report back to Gabriel and the others so we could form a plan."

"What others?" The pope asked cautiously.

"Oh, you know, Chris, Lucifer, Brennan, Aaron, and of course Gabriel. We left the other demons at home." I put my fisted hands on my hips.

"I do not know why Gabriel persists in working with the devil," the pope mused aloud.

"Maybe because, at least when it comes to current events, he's on the side of humanity."

The pope sighed and sank back down into the chair he'd been sitting in before. "You will bring them to us. There is an entrance they can utilize that will not attract notice. Sister Constance and Inquisitor Yashira will guide you."

I shivered. Inquisitor? That didn't sound good. I wasn't really in a position to complain, however, so I followed when the two women led me back out of the room everyone had been gathered in.

"And how did you fall in with the devil?" Yashira asked conversationally as we walked.

"Uh, well, I work for Chris and the whole apocalypse thing kind of involved a lot of us who otherwise would have just gone on living our lives serving people the best pizza in New Mexico. I'm here because the creature kidnapped me, and I offered to help since I was probably the only one in that group that wouldn't set off any wards when I came into the city."

The inquisitor snorted.

I glanced at her and noticed a faint smile on her lips. I supposed it was a little amusing.

"How did you end up with the inquisition. Isn't that, well, unexpected these days?"

Her expression blanked. "I was born to it."

That shut down the conversation, and I let it drop.

Instead of going back outside, Sister Constance took us down a side hallway then opened a freaking secret door. It was even behind an old, faded tapestry. I didn't see exactly what she did, other than pull aside the cloth. There was no real indication of a door. No seams in the dark wood. Nothing. But then she pushed, and the wall fell away silently.

"Wow," I breathed.

Instead of a flaming torch, she handed us all flashlights. Heavy industrial ones. She flipped hers on and it cast a yellow beam into the darkness. The sister went down the narrow stone steps first.

Clutching my light, I followed uneasily. Yashira brought up the rear.

The air was dank and the stone under my feet slippery, but I kept my footing. My relief at reaching the bottom of the long stairway was overshadowed by the oppressive darkness.

I didn't dare talk. I had no idea if we were safe down here or merely less likely to attract attention. Glancing back at the inquisitor let me see her stony face but gave me no clues as to how I should feel, and staring at the sister's back didn't help either.

Chris would totally have a wisecrack ready for a situation like this. Me? I just felt terrified. The close air and the cobwebs fluttering in the breeze from our passing didn't help.

Just when I thought I couldn't take the pressure of the unknown any longer, Sister Constance turned into an obscured side passage and led us back up another narrow, stone staircase.

Yashira's hand clamped down on my shoulder, startling a squeak out of me.

"You need to calm your breathing."

"Why?"

"So you don't pass out." Her tone made it clear how little she thought of me.

I gulped a few breaths and managed to get myself under a semblance of control. After another moment, the inquisitor let go of my shoulder and let me hurry after Sister Constance.

The nun waited for us at the top.

"Put out your lights," she ordered.

Unhappily, I did as she ordered. I heard a whisper of cloth and hoped that wasn't about to be my end. Instead of an attack, a crack of light appeared in the wall. She opened the door slowly to give our eyes time to adjust. I was still blinking in the brighter light when we came out into someone's root cellar. This was seriously like something out of a fantasy novel.

"Are we going to have company above?" I gestured at the ceiling.

"No. We own the property," Yashira replied. "All of the order currently in Italy are inside the Vatican either taken over by the demon or waiting for their chance to strike."

She made it sound like she didn't really care which, either. Which was not at all filling me with warm fuzzies. You know what would have given me warm fuzzies? My demon. I wanted to be wrapped up in his arms so badly right now.

Sister Constance took our flashlights and put them in a basket on a solid wooden shelf next to some potatoes.

My eyes finally adjusted. It wasn't that bright down here, just a single bare bulb in the low ceiling, but compared to the darkness of the passageway it had been bright.

We climbed an ancient wooden ladder up to another level then hurried out of the old home into the streets of Rome.

"Where are they?" Yashira took control of our group once we were outside.

Hesitantly, I named the hotel. I also pulled out my phone, that somehow had been returned to me, to give everyone a heads up that we were coming. Fortunately, I now had reception. Also, my battery was getting low, but I should be okay for a while longer. Stupid old battery.

Chris sent back a thumbs up to my text, and I had to hope that everything would go okay as I hurried after the Inquisitor and Sister Constance. My skin crawled and I stopped to glance over my shoulder and see if I could figure out what was bothering me. Not seeing anything, I turned to catch up to the others.

CHAPTER 25

Mandy

"**H**arrison, what are you doing?" I tugged futilely against his grip on my arms.

The vampire didn't answer me, just dragged me along behind a line of others as we traveled through the catacombs beneath Vatican City.

"Harrison, it's me, Mandy. Snap out of it!" I kicked backward, catching him in the shin.

I still wasn't clear on how I'd ended up down here. There was an unfortunately familiar blank in my memory between when I'd been following Yashira and the nun, but I suspected someone had grabbed me. That I woke up as quickly as I had was promising. Maybe I was getting better at resisting the creature's powers.

Something told me I really needed to escape before we got wherever we were being led. The people in front of me all seemed to be humans who had worked or served in the Holy City. Some were priests, many wore more common clothing. All shuffled along as if they were under someone else's control—which they were. Harrison was clearly also suffering from that condition.

Hoping to catch the vampire off guard, I collapsed to the ground and hoped he would drop me.

No such luck. I did make him trip over me, though and we ended up in a sprawl. I kicked out, catching him in the jaw with my foot. That got him to release me, and I scrambled to my feet, running back the way we'd come.

For a brief moment, I thought I might actually get away. Then Harrison slammed into my back, knocking me to the ground. The pain of hitting the dusty stone floor was nothing compared to the thought that I might have lost any chance I had with Harrison for good. Not to mention, I was probably going to die, too.

"What is going on here?"

I looked up and my blood ran cold. Those empty eyes were focused on me, and rage flickered in the depths of that soulless gaze.

"Let me go!" I shouted at the creature.

"No. You will draw the powerful ones to us. You are troublesome, but they keep coming, so you continue to serve." He reached down and jerked me to my feet with my t-shirt. I winced at the sound of ripping fabric.

"But you require submission." The creature's eyes reddened, and he bared long fangs. Not sexy fangs like Mal or Harrison had, but nasty, gross, death fangs that I wanted nowhere near me.

"Help me!" I screamed and kicked and prayed someone would answer my call.

Miraculously, someone did.

Again, I fell to the ground. This time, I landed on my feet as Harrison grappled with the creature. He'd broken free!

Their fight blocked my escape, so I fled the other direction, shoving past the humans in front of me. They shuffled to keep their balance but voiced no complaint. Heart pounding in my chest, I ran until someone tripped me. Then I went flying.

Bruised and defeated, I still tried to crawl away.

"Chain her," was all the creature said as it passed me, going to the head of the line.

Harrison must have appeased whatever rage the creature had toward me. He'd paid for my attempt at freedom. I had to believe he was still alive. I *needed* him to be alive.

Numb, I barely reacted when someone clamped cold iron around my wrists until they tugged, and I risked being dragged if I didn't get to my feet. I was already bruised enough, and now I had no hope of escaping. Only of rescue.

I wiped the tears from my cheeks and trudged along in the line of humans. He didn't seem to be very good at controlling my mind, but the chains worked well enough.

Mal and Chris would come for me. I was certain of it. Then they'd help me rescue Harrison because he *was* still alive. That thought helped me put one foot in front of the other. I just had to survive long enough for the others to find me. And this fucking monster would pay for hurting everyone.

CHAPTER 26

Price

"**W**ell, that's a turn of events I wasn't expecting," I said after relaying Mandy's text to my companions.

Lucifer had a shit-eating grin on his face. Gabriel remained impassive as did Brennan, though I sensed his resolve through our bond. Aaron felt nervous and tired, and I wondered if we should have left him behind. Still, having a half-angel around couldn't hurt anything. If nothing else, he shouldn't be in danger.

It didn't take long before someone knocked on the door. Mayhem growled softly, ruffling his fluffy yellow body, and staring at the door.

Brennan went and opened the door for us. On the other side was a very familiar-looking inquisitor and a nun.

I stepped forward. "Where's Mandy?" I said before anyone could say anything else.

Yashira and the nun shared a glance before the inquisitor turned back the way they had come to go search for Mandy.

"She was right with us," the nun replied after looking behind herself.

"Okay, but where is she now?" I persisted, hands curling into fists.

"I don't know," the nun cast her gaze to the floor.

"Please, come in," Gabriel finally said into the silence her statement brought.

"I'm Sister Constance." She pressed her hands together and bowed slightly toward Gabriel, clearly having a good idea of who they were.

"Hello, sister." Gabriel gestured a hand toward the others. "Our companions. The mage, Brennan. Chris Price, exorcist. Aaron, the Nephilim. And of course, The Adversary."

Sister Constance, to her credit, only paled a little and offered a polite bow. She even managed not to cross herself. I was impressed.

"We hear you are in a predicament," Lucifer said from where he sat on the couch, voice smooth with his normal levels of seduction. Not quite panty melting—he reserved that for me most of the time these days—but certainly full of promise.

"Yes, Adversary."

Lucifer chose not to press the issue with the nun. He was clearly enjoying himself, despite Mandy's absence.

Yashira returned shaking her head and frowning. "The child was with us the entire time. I swear it."

"Clearly not," I grumbled, pulling out my phone. I dialed Mandy but it rang through to voice mail. "Fuck."

Mayhem woofed softly, scenting the air before shaking his entire body and laying down by the door. I wasn't completely sure, but I thought he indicated that he did catch Mandy's scent.

"Come with us." Yashira pursed her lips unhappily. "We will be retracing our steps and perhaps we can find a clue."

"Mal has a pretty good finding spell." I glanced at Lucifer to see what he thought about the idea.

"He'll be in more danger than the rest of us," the devil pointed out.

"Malik has walked the halls of Heaven. He is welcome in our Holy City," Gabriel replied. "I simply did not think we would need him, or I would have included him in our party to begin with. I will retrieve the vampire."

Gabriel vanished without a goodbye.

"How has a vampire walked in Heaven?" Yashira asked, though her eyes widened probably at having voiced her question aloud.

"Eh, he was helping to save the world, and Gabriel took him and Sabian, my incubus, up to the heavenly library to do some research. Saved all our butts, so, good thing my vampire is a huge nerd."

The inquisitor took a deep breath, eyes shut, and jaw clenched, as if struggling with herself.

"Speaking of. You sure you're not working for this creature? Was pretty hard to tell whose side you were on the other day." I crossed my arms under my breasts and stared at the inquisitor.

"We are on the side of the Vatican."

"So, this creature gets control of your Holy City, and then you are on its side?"

"No, of course not," she spat.

Unfortunately, I couldn't do anything but keep an eye on her, so I didn't have an excuse to blast her with hellfire. The creature had wanted Mandy for bait, and it was possible he'd taken her again. I doubted she'd simply gotten lost.

Just then Gabriel returned with a wary-looking Mal in tow. Poor guy. He really hated how many people knew he was a vampire.

Yashira gave him an appraising glance but reserved comment. Sister Constance remained silent.

"Let us go to the others," Gabriel said. "You can perform your spell once we're inside the walls."

217

Mal shook his head. "I really hoped never to come back here."

I slapped him on the back. "Me too!"

Mayhem woofed as if in agreement.

Though I wanted to melt into Mal's arms, I refrained. Yashira took the lead.

I watched Mal and Mayhem scent the air once we were out on the streets. I could see the moment they both caught her scent. Mayhem's head snapped around, and Mal froze for a moment while they both considered what they'd discovered.

"Something grabbed her," Mal confirmed my fears. "Probably one of the creature's minions. I'm fairly certain she's inside the walls."

"Let's go." I gestured for Yashira to hurry.

The inquisitor didn't require further prompting. She hastened toward an old stone house near the wall around Vatican City. Old was relative in this country, but I was sure the house had stood for centuries. It was charming, well kept, and clearly ancient. I didn't take much time to look around as Yashira led us down a ladder into a root cellar. Not at all ominous, but we could defend ourselves.

In the cellar, Sister Constance took over. She moved a brick, and a shelf full of potatoes swung toward us. A black wall of nothing was behind it. It was almost like a portal, but not quite. No energy emanated from the opening, just dank cold. The nun handed out a few flashlights and into the darkness we went.

I shivered, imagining Mandy being put through all of this. I wanted to curse Gabriel and their willingness to put my employee in harm's way. It was one thing to send me, or any of my guys, but Mandy?

The creepier the tunnel got, the more annoyed I became. Gabriel should not have asked Mandy to do this. I should not have caved in so easily. Kicking myself as we walked, I almost missed the warning tingle as we got to the wards around Vatican City. Mal, who was right in front of me, stiffened before slowing and pushing through them. His reaction let me notice the warning tingle, and I braced myself. The burn was real, and far more than I'd experienced before. Had they done something to specifically target me? Or was it because I was lacking my bond with a certain fallen angel. Damn him, anyway.

Still, we passed through with only minor grumbles from a few of our members. Lucifer said nothing, and I wondered if the wards affected him, or not. Once we were across, we came to another staircase and climbed up. Though we'd had flashlights, the brightness in the room the next secret door opened into was almost painfully bright and it took a moment to adjust. Once I was able to see properly again, the narrow hallway we'd exited into had opened into a much more lavish corridor. Though, as I observed it more closely, it was devoid of a lot of the embellishments I'd seen in other parts of the Vatican.

Sister Constance led us to another room. Inside were a few other nuns, the pope and a few other priests, and one other man who looked like he might be an inquisitor like Yashira. Might even have been the guy my wards had tossed into the water.

Briefly, I wondered what had happened to the hunters, and if we needed to worry about them showing up, too. The way things were going the answer was yes.

The pope stood when they entered. Everyone else stood, as well, and Sister Constance and Yashira bowed.

Lucifer and the pope stared at each other, and the extended silence stretched, as they both waited for the other to begin.

I knew Lucifer would win this one. He had time. The pope didn't.

I was right. The pope finally bowed again.

"You were correct. I am asking for your help, Adversary. The creature has taken over many of our priests, our nuns, and the rest of the staff. He intends to unleash his people on the world."

I felt Sabian brush against my mind through our bond, and I turned my focus inward.

Chris, if you can, check out the American news.

I'll see what we can do. Love you.

I love you and miss you, and I can't wait to bend you over and...

Mate! I'm in the Vatican.

Sabian's sinfully delicious chuckle combined with his suggestion had my cheeks burning when I refocused on the conversation. Of course, they were all staring at me.

"Uh, yeah, we should check the news, I think. If we can get a signal."

The pope raised an eyebrow but gestured toward Yashira. She went around the table and pulled out a laptop and after a few clicks had one of the major American news sites up.

Pictures of semi-trucks parked across interstates and blocking bridges, and otherwise causing a massive disruption flashed across the screen. The scroller said something about the entire country being brought to a standstill by massive numbers of parked trucks.

"What the fuck?" I frowned.

"He was camped out at a truck stop for who knows how long," Mal pointed out. "Perhaps he hit some busier ones before he ended up in Wyoming stuck in a blizzard."

"Are they all vampires now?" I shuddered at the thought. New vampires would be hungry, and that many would be a huge problem.

"Let's hope not," Mal replied.

"According to literature," the pope said. "The creature is not able to create true vampire offspring but can control minds. Many of them and over vast distances. Supernatural creatures are harder to control, but he has many of them in his ranks, as well."

"So, these creatures are like, what, Renfield?" I wondered aloud.

"Yes," the pope answered.

"Creepy."

Yashira gave me a look I didn't quite get before she then glanced at Mal. If she was implying I did anything like eat bugs, I was going to punch her in the face. Before I could pursue that, Lucifer spoke.

"We will assist. Do you know of anything else that can aid us?"

"He has some resistance to the power of our faith," the pope admitted, though the flat tone of his voice suggested it pained him to do so. "And while it seems he's more interested in possessing others, he will kill if he thinks it necessary."

Yashira and the other inquisitor were glaring daggers at Lucifer. I guessed it was because of their friend who'd ended up in Hell. From what Lucifer had said, he deserved it anyway, so I didn't feel bad.

"You will take my inquisitors and defeat this creature." He hesitated. "Please."

Lucifer nodded. "Of course." He turned to Mal. "It is likely this creature has Mandy with him. Your tracking spell will be most useful."

Mal glanced around the room then lifted an eyebrow.

Lucifer shrugged, and my vampire sighed before going over to the table and pulling out his supplies. A map of the area he'd somehow acquired, his pendulum, and his knife. So Mal was going the blood magic route, again. Good for him. The holy folks could deal.

He glanced around one more time, shaking his head before drawing the knife across the pad of his thumb and letting a single drop slowly bead before it splattered onto the pendulum and vanished at a quiet word from Mal.

He didn't glance up when one of the inquisitors muttered something. I was sure he was doing a really solid job of ignoring them. The pendulum went straight over a building that wasn't the Papal Palace.

"So, what do you want to bet they're in the archive?" Mal muttered.

"I take it you've been there?" the pope said, dryly.

"No comment." Mal ran a hand through his hair.

Yashira snorted.

"It would be a logical place for them to go. Though the protections on the artifacts should keep most of the more dangerous objects out of the creature's hands," Lucifer said.

"It did not prevent a couple of demons from stealing one of the vilest books ever," the Pope replied. "Where did that end up, anyway?"

"I tossed it into a pit of hellfire and watched it burn," Lucifer replied.

"We have only your word on that," the pope countered, putting his palms flat on the table and staring at Lucifer.

"I witnessed," Gabriel spoke up for the first time in a while.

This caused the pope and the others a moment of silence.

"Also," Aaron finally spoke up a little belatedly. "They had my help when we got the book."

"Ahh," Pope John finally said. "Well, that explains much. Still, it's done, and I trust your demons will stay out of the archive in the future?"

Lucifer shrugged. "The future is a long time for promises. I guarantee you we have no current interest in it outside of present circumstances."

The pope inclined his head slightly.

"So, let's go?" I noted that the pope wasn't coming along on this adventure, but to be fair, he'd probably just slow us the fuck down, being an old human.

Yashira gestured toward the door.

"There is a back entrance. Sister Constance will guide you," Pope John said.

She didn't look happy about it, but she bowed slightly in acquiescence. We all followed the nun out into the hallway. She walked swiftly down another hallway and led us through another secret door.

Ten-year-old me was having a field day with all the secret doors. Adult me was freaking out a little because of the danger. I didn't want Mal anywhere near this vampire, but I didn't know that we had a lot of choice in the matter until we rescued Mandy.

I well remembered the expression in the creature's eyes when he looked at my vampire. He wanted Mal. And here we were, hopefully not delivering my vampire into his clutches.

We hurried through the dark tunnels, and I didn't pay much attention until Aaron, who had to walk stooped over much of the time, sucked in a breath. "Where are we?"

"These are some of the burial crypts in the catacombs," Sister Constance replied. "The ones we don't let the public know about, that is."

"Gotcha," I replied for all of us. We weren't going to tell anyone, anyway. I finally looked around. The area we walked through had widened and the ceiling was tall enough for Aaron to stand up in now. Though shadows obscured many of the details, I could see alcoves cut into the walls where skeletons rested.

Something skittered along one. Rats. I grimaced and wondered if they kept any cats down here to hunt.

Something else moved in the shadows, and I halted. Mayhem growled softly.

Lucifer, who walked behind me, put a hand on my shoulder, and I pointed.

Mal came to a sudden stop as well, and Sister Constance took a few more steps before she realized the rest of us weren't moving. I was actually surprised I'd noticed the movement before my vampire, but he was concentrating on his spell.

"You might as well show yourselves," I said into the silence, broken until then only by a few shuffles from Aaron and quiet breathing from all the humans.

A woman stepped from the shadows. "Becca?" I guessed after a moment.

She nodded.

"Where are the rest of you?"

"The creature has them."

Lucifer squeezed my shoulder gently, letting me know he thought she was telling the truth.

"Well, you should probably join us then. We're on a rescue and destroy mission ourselves."

"What are you destroying?" She moved to join us, giving Mal a wary look.

I stifled a laugh. He really wasn't the one she needed to worry about.

"The creature. Hopefully."

"We haven't found a way for him to be killed. Incapacitated, yes, but not killed."

"We will capture and take him to Hell," Lucifer said. "If we can't kill him, we can imprison him in a way he won't escape."

If he meant the soul traps, yeah, the creature wouldn't get out of one of those. Death would be a kindness, in that case. I'd almost been trapped in one a few months ago and hoped never to repeat the experience.

Becca studied Lucifer. "How are you getting him to Hell?"

I snorted. "Did Perl not tell you of her little trip we took together?"

"She was vague on the details."

"Well, we have our ways. Let's go." We'd delayed enough.

Sister Constance hurried on at my gesture, and we all followed. When we came to a junction, Sister Constance and Mal conferred before picking a direction.

Time stretched in the unending catacombs, and I felt like we had been down here for an eternity. It had probably only been an hour, but it felt like ages.

Finally, we stopped. Sister Constance put her hand on a raised stone. "This will let you out into the archive. I will not go with you. I think you know your way."

Mal grimaced and nodded.

"I have also been here, before," Lucifer said. "As has Gabriel."

At the mention of the angel's name, Becca's eyes widened, and she stared at the child-like being.

I guessed she hadn't figured out who Lucifer was, either.

"Very well. Good luck." She hesitated before continuing. "May God guide your steps."

Lucifer refrained from sarcasm, but I could practically feel the effort it took for him to keep his mouth shut.

Gabriel shot the devil an amused look in a rare display of emotion.

Sister Constance opened the door for us, and we hurried through. I'd thought we would go up. Though it seemed like we were on one of the upper floors of a circular room and when I went over to the edge, it just went down and down and down.

"Fuck," I muttered. "Didn't they believe in handrails?"

"It's very impressive," Lucifer agreed. "And apparently not."

Aaron sighed. "I really don't like this place."

Mal slapped Aaron on the back. "Agreed."

"So, any idea where we go from here?" I didn't want to know the answer, but I suspected it was down.

Lucifer and Gabriel both glanced over the edge before confirming my fears. "Down," the devil replied.

"So, uh, is there a quick way?" We did not have all day, and I couldn't even really make out the bottom in the dim lighting.

"We, uh, used powers," Aaron said into the silence my question brought.

"Yashira?"

"We have never been here before," she replied, for once sounding at a loss.

"I will lower us." Gabriel waved their hand in front of them, and a golden glow formed over the edge of the pit. They stepped onto it and turned to face us.

Swearing under my breath, I followed and didn't look down. Quite a leap of faith as Gabriel could fly. If they were looking for a quick way to end the Price bloodline, letting me fall would do it. Though I suspected Mayhem would have stopped me if I'd truly been in danger. Not to mention several of my guys had pretty serious magical abilities. I was probably safe even if Gabriel wanted me dead. Maybe.

As if sensing my thoughts, the archangel gave me a considering stare. I shrugged.

The others, seeing that I didn't fall, got onto Gabriel's floating golden light. As soon as we were onboard, he let it sink toward the depths.

"So, I feel like we're just going to drop right into the middle of a fight. We should be ready." I glanced down, finally. I couldn't really see into the gloom, but far below I thought I saw some flickering lights.

Instead of answering, Lucifer drew his sword from wherever it magically stayed when he wasn't using it. Purple flames licked along the blade. I'd wielded that blade on several occasions, and my fingers tingled with the memory of its power. My devil glanced at me, as if sensing my thoughts, or outright listening in. He smiled and offered me the sword. I adamantly shook my head. As much as the power called to me, I didn't want everything that came with it. Lucifer winked.

Gabriel also drew their sword, and white flames flickered along the blade.

Seeing everyone else draw their swords, Aaron pulled his out as well.

The others also armed themselves, and I got ready to cast magic and sling snark. A shout went up from below us. Shit! Something spotted us.

Becca's eyes were wide as she stared at Lucifer's sword. "I don't know that we've been properly introduced. I thought you were one of the exorcist's men, but…" She waved at his sword, which matched Gabriel's closely in design.

"Ahh, but I am one of Chris's men," Lucifer replied with a panty-melting grin.

"The Adversary is partially responsible for this creature's escape. I also carry some of the blame. Therefore, we will see it destroyed, or imprisoned," Gabriel explained.

Becca blanched then stared at me. "You're fucking the devil?"

I shrugged. "Gabriel assures me it's not a sin."

That actually got the archangel to laugh. "I never said that, Chris Price. I simply affirmed that your soul was not tainted."

"Close enough."

The look Yashira and the other inquisitor gave me was really not worth noticing, so I ignored them. I was happy with my decisions, even if they were a little strange.

The magical lift slowed and vanished, dropping us all an inch or so to the floor. I'd been distracted on the way down, but now we stood at the bottom of the archive, and I glanced around. The space was surprisingly large, and relics stood in several alcoves with golden glows around them. Magic. Probably those sticky traps that Aaron and Ezra had tangled with. They obscured the relics somewhat, though one of the alcoves was suspiciously empty, and I guessed that was where the grimoire had been housed.

The creature and many of his minions gathered around the edges of one of the alcoves, all staring at someone who had just been tossed into one of the sticky traps. Instead of slowing the being down, the creature seemed to accelerate until it slammed into one of the spikes coming off the weapon protected by the magic. When the being slammed into it, he screamed, red lines bursting through his skin. He then disintegrated in a cloud of ash that the spell blasted into the far wall. A wall that was greasy with fresh ash.

How many beings had he thrown in there?

A line of people, probably mostly human, though I saw a few that looked like they might be supernatural, stood with blank expressions. I recognized Asher, Perl, Gael, and, of course, Mandy. She, unlike the others, was staring at us with clear eyes and a pleading expression. She was chained. The creature must have grabbed her out from under Yashira and the nun's noses.

The creature stood near the line. When the last of the prisoner's screams faded, he snatched another of the humans and tossed them into the trap, with similar results.

"Yeah, we probably don't want him getting hold of that I'm guessing?" I couldn't watch this any longer. I had to do something.

"No, my dear. We do not." Lucifer shifted his grip on his sword.

The shouts clearly hadn't been aimed at us at all. None of the creatures even noticed us until I spoke.

They turned, and the creature screamed in rage. His vacant eyes were no longer vacant when he looked at us, and they chilled me to the bone.

"Get them," the thing hissed.

Twisted creatures, probably once vampires, demons, and other supernatural beings sprang from all directions. Yashira and the other inquisitor charged into the battle, prayers on their lips and bullets flying from their—thankfully—suppressed guns. Gabriel, Lucifer, and Aaron waded into the fray with their swords, while Brennan and I wielded magic. Mayhem, now in his full hellhound glory, tore into our attackers. Mal used the distraction to rescue Mandy.

Dakota Brown

CHAPTER 27

Mandy

I'd never been more relieved to see my boss than when she appeared out of nowhere with a bunch of other people. I knew she'd come for me. I had just hoped she'd get here before the creature murdered me. Or worse. He'd been happy to inform me that I was bait, this time and before in Wyoming. He'd also given me a glimpse of his plans for me once the others were under his control. I shied away from those thoughts.

Mal scrambled toward me when the others engaged in battle.

"I'm so sorry you keep having to save me," I blurted out.

"None of that, Mandy," he whispered. His low, soothing, undeniably sexy accent put me at ease. I was almost convinced everything was going to be okay. He snapped the iron manacles on my wrists like they were nothing, sending a small surge of something through me. Probably lust, but I wasn't going to follow that train of thought very far.

He gathered me into his arms, and we raced away from the others.

"Aaron, can you get them out of here?" Chris shouted.

Aaron, who looked magnificent with his double set of wings fully manifested, a white glow surrounding him, and his sword gleaming in the low light, nodded.

"Damn, Aaron," I murmured from Mal's arms.

The half-angel spared me a quick smile before he released his sword. It vanished.

"Mal?" he asked in his deep rumbly voice.

"If you take Mandy, I can get out of here nearly as quickly. Then I can help her escape, and you can return to the fight." Mal twisted his lips in annoyance.

"I want out of here!" I exclaimed, my voice squeaking with my terror.

Mal chuckled before handing me into Aaron's arms. Before I could even begin to feel awkward about it, he launched himself into the air and we were flying.

"Oh my god, this is amazing," I breathed. The experience banished some of the terror I'd felt before, and I was grateful for it.

Aaron flashed me another quick smile. "You're welcome, Mandy."

In only a few moments, we landed gently on one of the top levels. I didn't see what Mal did, but Aaron had barely helped me to my feet when he appeared next to us.

The two men exchanged a quick hug, and then Aaron dove off the edge, back into the fight.

"We have to find Harrison," I pleaded. "He's here somewhere."

"He wasn't down there?"

I shook my head. "No, he was fighting back against the creature after it took me again, and they dumped him somewhere. He tried to save me!"

Mal clenched his jaw.

"Please, Mal. He's a friend. He's helped both me and Warrick a few times now. He distracted the creature from taking out his frustrations on me when they took me again. We have to save him."

The last decided Mal, though he sighed when he nodded. "Let's get out of here, first. Then we'll search for your friend."

"Thank you."

He led me from the archive and into one of the many passages before we stopped.

"I don't know Harrison, so I'm going to need your help for this tracking spell." He pulled out his map and pendulum. "Think of him as strongly as you can and hold this pendulum."

I did as he instructed. Mal took my other hand and touched the knife to the pad of my thumb. "Just a drop."

I nodded, holding everything I could in my mind that reminded me of Harrison, including Warrick's insistence that we should fuck.

Mal's knife was sharp, and I didn't even feel the cut until he squeezed a drop of blood on the pendulum. I watched in fascination as it vanished at a quiet word from Mal. The pendulum tugged, strongly, and the urge to follow it was just as strong.

I looked at my thumb and the line of blood before holding out my hand. "I don't think Chris will get mad at you."

He shook his head. "No, she won't. And you shouldn't have an open wound. Certainly not under these circumstances, anyway." He took my hand and quickly flicked his tongue across my wound, closing it with his vampire powers.

I bit my lip, trying really hard not to react. Mal winked then tugged on my hand. "Let's go find your vampire."

Mal grabbed my hand and used his superior vampire vision to guide us through the darkness. My nearly dead cell phone wouldn't be much use as a flashlight, anyway.

233

Though he did eventually pull out his own cellphone and flipped on the flashlight when I kept tripping.

We ran as quickly as I could manage, with Mal dragging me along, until he dropped my hand and drew a sword strapped to his back. How had I not seen that? Magic?

Moments later, I heard what had alerted Mal. The scuff of footsteps on stone sent chills down my spine. I glanced at the pendulum. It pointed down a different corridor, but something told me that we didn't want whoever that was behind us, either.

Mal shoved his phone at me. "Go, Mandy. I'll catch up."

I wanted to protest. I really did. Instead, I did what I was told and ran. I couldn't help Mal anyway, and I might slow him down.

Following the pendulum, I sprinted as fast as I could away from the fight, trying not to let fear turn my legs to jelly, even when I heard the clang of steel on steel.

***

I felt my way along the wall, one hand held high in front of my face so I didn't smack my head on something, and one hand trailing against the stone. In some places the wall was smoother, in some rough. Some places had cutouts and others were oddly rounded and brittle feeling. Except for the oddly rounded places, it all felt like cold stone. I couldn't see except when I pulled my phone out and used it as a flashlight. My battery was low, and I was trying to reserve the power for when I really needed it. Like at intersections. Mal's phone had died already, and I had it tucked in my back pocket. I'd left him a small eternity ago, and I tried not to think about what it might mean that he hadn't rejoined me yet.

My footsteps were loud on the stone floor, and I swore I could hear my heart beating over my harsh breaths.

I cursed the asshole who had dumped Harrison out here. I just wished I knew where I was. Well, I knew where I was. I just didn't know where anything else happened to be, or how to get out.

I'd have a much better chance of getting out of this if I could find Harrison. Assuming I could help him if he were hurt, or the creature hadn't broken his mind again. This would be a lot easier if Mal would catch up to me.

I found another crossroads and scooted backward until my hand rested on one of the strange, curved brittle feeling pieces of the wall. Then I turned on the flashlight on my phone. A quick glance at the pendulum Mal had given me led straight ahead. I tucked it back in my pocket then glanced at the wall. Holy fuck, that was a skull. I'd been running my hand along old skulls. Moaning, I made myself refocus on my task and turned my flashlight off after a mournful look at the red power bar. I was almost out. I had to find Harrison before I ran out of power.

Going as fast as I dared, I hurried down the corridor. My foot caught on something, and I went sprawling. I caught myself, but my wrist shrieked in pain, and I was afraid to look at it, because I was pretty sure I'd broken it.

"Damn it!" I practically shouted, not caring who might hear. I was going to die down here because my battery on my phone was older than dirt and wouldn't hold a charge anymore and Mal had gotten into trouble, and I couldn't help him, and I couldn't help me. "Fuck!" I added for good measure, though that was more Chris's swear word than mine.

Using my less injured hand, I fumbled for my phone and managed to get the light back on. I steadfastly did *not* look at my other wrist and ignored the pain shooting through me. At this point, it was the least of my worries and that gave me some ability to disregard the pain.

"Well, that's less shitty," I murmured. The thing I'd tripped over was Harrison's leg.

Of course, he had a stake driven through his heart and was unconscious. Because of course he was. Poor guy had been staked twice now in the last few weeks.

There was really only one outcome to this scenario. I was going to lose some blood. Hopefully not all of it. Hopefully, he'd come around enough to give me some back and heal my hurts. I wasn't ready to die, but if I didn't wake Harrison up, I'd probably die anyway. I couldn't afford to wait for Mal. He might not be coming. I shied away from that thought, but I seriously would have thought he'd have found me by now.

The words that Warrick had said came back to me.

"Save Harrison if you can. Get him to join us if you want."

"Oh?"

Warrick had winked. "I want him. You want him. Win-win."

That got my eyes to widen. "Okay. I'll do what I can."

"He wants you, too."

We hadn't had a chance to continue the conversation at that time. It was relevant now, so I was glad we'd had it. I knew what a vampire's bite did and I was certainly not so strong that if my nearly lifelong adult fantasy literally bit me in the neck, I'd be able to resist hitting that.

I could wish for better surroundings, but then again, the Roman catacombs were amusing, if nothing else.

"Harrison, I don't know if you can hear me, but if you can, know this: yes, I want to have sex with you, please don't hurt my wrist more, and please don't kill me." I paused, considering the order I'd said those statements in.

Maybe my priorities were a little off, but he wasn't going anywhere until I pulled the stake out.

Hoping this wasn't the last thing I did, I kneeled on the vampire's chest and gripped the stake with my less injured hand and yanked. Unlike last time, this stake came out a little easier. I fell back, but before I could hit the floor, Harrison was on me.

"Oh, I forgot one! You can have my blood, just not all of it!" I hurriedly blurted as his teeth sank into my neck. "Oh, hell," I gasped as the brief snap of pain was replaced by crashing pleasure that tore relentlessly through me. It was almost painful, but my body gave in to the insistent pressure, and it was almost like my entire being orgasmed, even my mind, as my fantasy became reality.

The feeling of his teeth in my neck, the pressure as he drew my blood from me, the weight of him holding me, and the exquisite ecstasy as the venom in his bite forced me to pleasure like I'd only even glimpsed at Warrick's hands, was everything I had dreamed of, and more. Warrick was good, but he'd been holding back on some of his powers for fear of hurting me. I suspected Harrison would have held back too if he'd been in control.

I was floating in an endorphin induced high, my body languid, accepting orgasm after orgasm as if they were its due.

The blackness at the edges of my vision was mildly concerning. The only thing that really broke through that haze was the musical chime as my phone died and my light went out for good.

Harrison growled, the sound going straight to my groin. My body spasmed again.

Somehow, I knew if he didn't stop soon, I wouldn't live to repeat this experience, but I was beyond caring.

"Mandy?"

"Hmm?" I slurred.

"Balls. Mandy!"

"Just heal me and then fuck me," I murmured.

"Warrick is going to kill me!"

"Naw, wants you to fuck me, too." I giggled, truly drunk on his bite.

Harrison didn't reply, just put his wrist to my mouth. A few drops of salty, coppery liquid dropped on my tongue, and I swallowed reflexively.

The bite was nothing compared to what his blood did to me. When I finally swam my way out of the drunken haze, Harrison was staring at me uneasily.

"Wait, how can I see you?"

"I had my phone. No cell reception but my battery isn't dead."

"Great, can we fuck now?"

His eyebrows rose. "You're serious?"

"The only thing that could make this night better is for you to do all of that to me again, but this time, also stuffed full of your cock." I tried to smile seductively. It probably just came across as drunken. Everything he'd just done to me had completely driven the horrors of the last few days out of my mind.

"Warrick…"

"And I talked. We both want this."

"Don't you want to get out of here first? We can certainly do the cock stuffing thing more comfortably in a bed." He was grinning now, obviously amused.

"Wait, you're not under their control anymore?"

Harrison shook his head. "Broke it. Again. Which is why I ended up staked and down here. I think that might be why I got staked the last time, too. And I'll know how to avoid it in the future."

"Oh, good. So…" My hand went to my jeans.

Harrison licked his lips, and I think he was about to agree when something crashed in the distance. We both stiffened.

"Later," we said in unison, and we scrambled to our feet.

I stared back the way I'd come, then in the other direction, torn. I had no idea how to get out of here. When I glanced at Harrison, he shrugged. "No idea. I was unconscious."

"Shit."

Another crash made both of us jump. Then one of the most welcome sights came into view. At least for me.

"Fuck me," Harrison shouted, frantically searching around for a place to hide.

Mal sprinting into the faint beam of light from Harrison's phone with his sword drawn made me pretty happy.

"Mal!"

"Chris and the others are working on taking down the creature, but his minions are still under his control and they're coming this way. We should run."

"You're not going to cut my head off?" Harrison backed a step away.

"Only if you hurt Mandy," he replied.

Harrison swallowed. "You didn't say you had an ancient ass vampire big brother."

Mal chuckled. "She does. Now, let's go before I have to cut off more heads. They think that once the creature is destroyed, most of the people he controls will be savable. I'd rather not kill them if I don't have to."

"Lead the way!" I gestured for Mal to take control.

He gave one last long look at Harrison before running ahead.

Harrison gave me another wide-eyed look before taking my arm and pulling me along behind Mal. With his help we were able to move fairly quickly. It seemed like Mal knew where he was going, too, because before long he had us running up a narrow staircase and out into an impossibly bright, extremely ornate hallway. Gilded things, marble pillars, suits of armor, works of art, all of these flashed past me as I ran with the two vampires. Mal didn't even slow, so we were clearly not out of danger yet.

CHAPTER 28

Brennan

I'd had more than enough fighting to last many lifetimes, but here we were again. At least this time the angels and demons were on our side. It seemed like the creature had put endless hordes of his people down here. They spilled out of the shadows, some armed, some not, coming at us with everything they had.

Knowing that we might be able to save some of these people later had me attempting to disable instead of kill, but it was hard with as furious as the battle was.

Gabriel and Lucifer cut swaths through the beings, trying to get at the creature. Chris and Mayhem were at their side. The inquisitors and the hunter fought to free their people, while Aaron and I kept us all from being overrun from behind. The fighting was a chaotic mess, and I wished that we had brought Ezra and his powerful magic along, though I knew he'd have been at a huge disadvantage in the fight. He had to be freaking out about now as we could all feel Chris pulling on her well of power.

No sooner had I thought about Ezra than a jagged black line ripped through the middle of our battlefield, and the demon prince and a horde of hellhounds burst out of the portal. It snapped shut much faster than normal, probably taking everything he had to open it, especially directly here. Likely only his connection to Chris and Lucifer had allowed it.

The baying of the hellhounds deafened me for a moment, but I had never been gladder to see a demon or demonic dogs other than Mayhem.

The tide of the battle turned quickly, and we pushed the minions back into the depths of the archive where they'd come from, freeing Lucifer and Gabriel and Chris to take on the creature.

I liked it less that the two inquisitors were also at Chris's side, but so far, they'd behaved.

Lucifer snarled something at the creature and froze the thing with his demonic power. Gabriel advanced at his side, and it appeared that they had control and we'd won.

Though I didn't relax my spells, I felt a bit of the tension leaving my shoulders.

Too soon. The creature, though captured, retained enough mobility to reach out his hand toward the female inquisitor. She jerked as if she were now a puppet, grabbed Chris, and with inhuman strength, tossed her into the magical trap around the weapon they'd been trying to retrieve.

"No!" I shouted.

Lucifer bellowed the same word, tossed his sword at Gabriel and dove in after her.

I didn't catch what Gabriel said as they caught the demonic sword, but it was too late. Lucifer had somehow caught Chris and twisted so he was between her and the weapon. I felt a massive draw of power and their progress toward the weapon slowed, however it didn't stop completely.

Mayhem howled in rage, launching himself at Yashira and ripping out her throat. The inquisitor crumpled to the ground, though I doubted she'd been in control of herself at the time. Still, she'd probably wanted to kill Chris and Lucifer, so I didn't feel too bad for her.

Mayhem didn't go after Chris. He paced at the edge of the trap, breathing hellfire into it. The hellfire didn't do anything to dispel the magic. I was shocked he didn't go after her. Maybe he understood that he would just be trapped, too.

The only one of us who managed to keep an eye on the objective was Gabriel. They took over Lucifer's hold on the creature, keeping him from escaping.

"Prince Ezra," Gabriel said into the resounding silence that followed. "I require that you take up your master's sword so we may end this creature."

Ezra had to wrench his horrified gaze away from the spectacle of Chris and Lucifer suspended in the trap, slowly inching their way closer to the spiked weapon and death.

"What do I need to do?" he asked, his voice hoarse.

"Simply plunge the blade in at the same time I do and lend me your demonic magic. I believe together the powers of Heaven and Hell will defeat this being."

Reluctantly, Ezra accepted Lucifer's sword, wincing slightly as he took hold of it.

The creature struggled, but ultimately, he was no match for the archangel. Between my magic, Aaron, and the hellhounds we were easily able to keep the minions away.

Together, Gabriel and Ezra plunged their swords into the creature's chest. It let out an awful, inhuman scream and burst into flames. I could feel Gabriel manipulating energies at a level I had no hope of ever achieving. Not if I wanted to remain sane, anyway.

Ezra lent Gabriel all the power the angel required as they contained the fires from the creature until it had burned out and died. Then both he and Ezra dismissed the swords. Gabriel sank to their knees, and Ezra, well, he melted into the shadows that clung to the air around us. I'd not seen him do this before, but I'd heard about it from the others when they'd finally told me about how they'd retrieved the book that held the spell necessary to save Chris's life a few months ago.

The minions all collapsed, and a wave of exhaustion rolled over me as I let the magic go. I rushed forward to see if there was any way I could help save Chris, but she and Lucifer had vanished.

Frantically, I searched for our connection. I would have felt it if she'd died, wouldn't I? No, it was still there, faint as if she were unbelievably distant, but still there. Had Lucifer been killed? Was she reinstated as the ruler of Hell? Mayhem had also vanished, I noted belatedly.

"Gabriel, what happened to them?" Aaron demanded before I could find the words.

Ezra reappeared and offered the archangel a hand back to their feet. Surprisingly, they accepted.

"I do not know. I need a moment to recover. That being was stronger than even I anticipated."

They gazed down at the dead inquisitor, her white suit stained red with her blood. The hunters had all survived and they joined us, eyes wide, but they were seasoned warriors and once they'd been freed, had done their part in this fight.

We all looked at Ezra. He shook his head, then groaned, putting his hands to his temple as if regretting the motion. "I'm only a demon prince. I can barely sense myself, let alone anything else after that," he managed to get out.

"We should retreat," Gabriel said. "By the time we've cleared this place of unwanted guests, and returned to the pope, I will have recovered my full abilities, and I will be able to tell you what has happened to the exorcist and the Adversary."

Unhappy with the plan, but not sure what else to do for the moment, I nodded acceptance and tried to turn my thoughts from the worst and instead hope for the best. It was, after all, Chris Price, and she had never yet let one of her men stay dead for very long.

Dakota Brown

CHAPTER 29

Price

"Fuck!" I shouted as that damn Yashira grabbed me and tossed me into the trap. She was fast and even my wards didn't trip before the magic contained the blast that otherwise would have thrown her away from me. She hadn't directly harmed me, and that might have let her slip through the protections. They weren't perfect.

There was nothing I could do, though I scrabbled for my magic, trying to shield myself, or something. Maybe the wards would protect me from the spikey death weapon? They were practically my only hope.

That was until someone grabbed me and spun me around. I felt an astronomical surge of energy, and my progress through the spell slowed to a crawl. Lucifer had somehow grabbed me and spun us until he was between me and the weapon.

"What are you doing?" I tried to say, but the spell stole my words, and no sound came out.

Lucifer jerked my mind away to the white space we'd once shared to communicate while he'd been dwelling in my body.

"My dear, you should portal us out of here," he said, his voice strained.

"Can't you? My portals are shit."

"It is taking everything I have to slow this infernal spell down."

"Please tell me that spikey-ass weapon won't hurt angels and, you know, fallen ones."

Lucifer grimaced. "I'll be very, permanently dead, if you don't get us out of here."

"Why would you do that! You have to rule Hell. You can't risk yourself. Even for me!" I snarled at him.

"I love you, Chris Price. There is nothing I would not risk to save you. Please, portal us out of here so that I may replace my mark upon your chest, and you may reclaim me with your own." The seduction in his voice was overlain by the strain of keeping us alive. Before I could call him all sorts of creative names for being such a huge dumbass, we snapped back into our bodies, and I saw just how close we'd come to that weapon. It was inches from Lucifer's back. His eyes were closed as he held me tightly by the arms.

There was enough space that I could place a portal between his back and the weapon. But... I didn't think we could make portals here. That was the entire point of all the fancy protections, to keep people from doing exactly that and making off with all the nasty things down here.

Chris!

I grabbed for my magic. The necessary spell slipped through my fingers. It wasn't even that I sucked at portals. I really was better than your average person at them, just not as good as someone like Lucifer who'd been doing them for centuries. It was the wards preventing me from doing what I wanted.

I needed his power for this. Since I was moving in the direction the spell wanted, I was able to reach out and grab his forearm. I formed the spell for my own version of a demon mark and planted it on his forearm, just as I had before.

The surge of energy that burned through me was too much. Once, I'd held it all, and more, and it had nearly burned me out. Lucifer's gasp and his frantic jerk away from the spikes we were being inexorably dragged toward, pulled me out of my hesitation. I accepted everything, let it burn through me, and formed the portal moments before we would have been auditioning for a new ruler of Hell.

We crashed through it as he let go of whatever he had been doing to slow our passage through the trap, and we spilled out of the portal into one of my favorite rooms in his domain. His study, with the hearth and the fur rug that I loved to lay on. Lucifer gasped out a breath as I landed on him, his eyes snapping open as he slowly realized he wasn't actually dead.

"Do you really love me?" I asked once he was focused on me.

Lucifer clutched me against him. "Yes, Chris, I do very much. I love you more than life itself."

"Oh. Good. Because I love you, too." I grabbed his face and pressed my lips against his.

We kissed until I was gasping for breath, and then he flipped us until I was under him. He pressed his hand to my chest and his power once again burned through me, igniting a fire deep in my core that we both felt through our restored bonds.

Somewhere in there, our clothing vanished, and we gave into our need to be connected in every way possible. I never again wanted to be separated from this man I loved.

"The creature! Uh, should we have gone back?"

Lucifer stared at me in disbelief. "And miss all this?"

"I mean…" I knew my guys were fine, but I suddenly felt bad.

"They'd handled the creature by the time we escaped," Lucifer said, trailing his fingers over my stomach as he traced the sigils he and the others had marked on my skin.

"Oh, good!" I dragged Lucifer back down to me and we lost ourselves in each other again. The rest of the world could wait.

CHAPTER 30

Lucifer

I watched my exorcist sleep from the couch, grateful that I'd finally gotten over my hang-ups and replaced our bonds. I longed to rejoin her, but I'd sensed Gabriel and assumed they were going to chew me out for bonding with Chris again. Or worse, for having almost sacrificed myself for her. Sighing, I got up and magicked on a pair of pants.

"Adversary," Gabriel said by way of greeting as they manifested next to me.

"Gabriel." I liked the angel, I really did. They could have waited until later, though.

"You are both well?"

I nodded.

"Good." They turned as if to leave.

"That's it?"

"What else is there to say?"

I gestured at Chris. Though she was covered, they would be able to see the mark with his angelic sight.

"Lucifer, you and Chris went into this bonding knowing what you were getting into. You deserve to love and be loved. So does she. Enjoy your peace for as long as it may last."

"That's not ominous. Is something coming?"

Gabriel shook their head. "I cannot see beyond this moment. Peace may last for lifetimes. It may last for moments. I simply wish for you to enjoy the peace while you have it. She is tied into your power and Ezra's. You will have lifetimes together. Some of it will be turbulent. Some not." Gabriel clasped their hands together in front of them.

Belatedly, I realized they'd called me by my name for the first time since I'd willingly fallen from Heaven.

"So, I'll be seeing you soon?"

"Unfortunately, it is likely. Chris Price is as much a magnet for trouble as you are. I will reassure the others, then return to Heaven."

"My thanks, old friend."

Gabriel smiled. "Adversary."

This time they left through the door, and I returned to the nest we'd made in front of the fire, wrapping myself around my exorcist and feeling complete for the first time in quite a while.

CHAPTER 31

Mandy

Meeting the pope had been… something. Especially as I'd been accompanied by two vampires. Somehow, he'd known right away what Harrison was, and he'd already known Mal.

Still, he'd been gracious enough to me though we'd all waited in somewhat uncomfortable silence until finally the others had returned with Gabriel. Though Chris and Lucifer had been missing. The child-like angel had a brief conversation with the pope then transported all of us back to Chris's living room, where I'd immediately thrown myself into Warrick's arms.

Gabriel had vanished, saying they were going to check on Chris and Lucifer, then returned long enough to tell us that they were okay, then vanished again. Probably back to Heaven or wherever angels hung out when they weren't fighting ancient evil creatures.

I hadn't left Warrick's arms. Harrison stood close by me shooting nervous glances at both Warrick and Mal.

Once everyone had settled, Mal had given us all a ride over to my apartment. After another warning to Harrison not to hurt me, he left us.

And now we were in my apartment, and I remembered we had a giant bathtub.

"I'm disgusting!" I did my best exhausted attempt at a run, while shedding my clothing.

Warrick, bless him, had the tub magically filled by the time I reached it, and it was, of course, the perfect temperature. I scrambled ungracefully over the side and almost fell into the warm pool of lightly scented water.

My incubus was not far behind.

"Uh, so, uh, mind if I use the shower then?" Harrison stammered, his hot British accent thicker with his embarrassment.

"You should join us," Warrick said.

"Uh, you know, I don't want to intrude on what you two have going on. It's clearly very special."

"Ahh, Harrison, you have no idea how much Mandy wants you," Warrick said. "But I do because I'm an incubus and I can read her thoughts on the matter. And I also know you want her very much. Now here's the really cool part. I like sex, I like my partners to be happy, and while I'm not willing to share the love of my life with just anyone, you are worthy. So, I want you to join us, too."

Harrison's jaw dropped a little before he snapped it shut. "I mean, she said as much, but I didn't really believe anyone would be willing to share someone as delightful as Mandy."

His words made me melt a little bit.

Warrick slid his hand up my thigh and I felt a trickle of his energy roll through me. I groaned as it lit me up from the inside. Harrison's nostrils flared.

"Or as delicious smelling."

"So, our Mandy here, she has always had a thing for vampires. We all know she has a tiny crush on Mal. She's really excited to have met you, but, and yes, I know I'm speaking for her right now, she also likes you for who you are, not just your pointy teeth."

Harrison had to snap his jaw shut again.

"So, it's up to you." Warrick patted the water.

I smiled invitingly at Harrison and ran my hand over my breasts. "I'd like it if you would join us. But only if you want. Don't, like, you know, feel pressured." I dropped my hand.

"Oh, I want to, luv. This is just new territory for me."

"Me too!" I tried to sit up so I could look at him more directly and slipped, ruining the effect as I splashed and choked on the water.

Harrison gripped me under the arms and hauled me upright.

"You okay, luv?"

"Just, you know, been a long few days and I'm not as smooth as normal." I giggled. "I'm never smooth. So, anyway, if you'd rather rest, you can crash in my room. Warrick and I will make a nest out here."

Harrison snorted. "Super hearing, super smell, there's no way I'd be able to rest. I'll join you, if you're sure."

"Yes. I'm sure." I grinned when Harrison pulled his t-shirt over his head.

He wasn't built like Warrick was, tall, muscular, solid. He was, however, defined. He had a lovely V on his front I was dying to explore, and though it was lean, he had plenty of muscle to drool over.

He hesitated again when his hand went to his fly.

"Do you want me to not devour you with my eyes while you undress?" I licked my lips humorously.

Harrison bit his lip. "I mean, I'm nothing to look at compared to Warrick, there."

"Seriously?" I scrambled out of the tub and almost fell on my face again.

Harrison was quick enough to save me, and I plastered myself against him. The need between my legs grew as my breasts rubbed against his bare chest.

He nuzzled my neck, inhaling deeply. "Mmm, you smell delicious, Mandy."

"And you look delicious." It was a dumb reply, but it did the trick.

Harrison kissed my neck, and I nibbled at his collarbone.

"Fuck, luv."

"That's the idea. Can I?" My hands went to the button on his pants.

"Yeah, go ahead."

I did my best to make it sexy, but I wasn't exactly good at stripping myself, let alone someone else. Still, I got his pants undone and slid them down his thighs, going to my knees in front of him as I did.

His hands on my shoulders trembled as I stood back up, rubbing my chest along his cock.

Harrison groaned.

"So, get in the bath, because we're all kinda gross, and I want to fuck, but not until we've washed the last few days off."

He didn't require any further prompting, and soon we had devolved into a game of splashing each other with bubbles and giggling until I felt we were clean enough. Then Warrick did more amazingly useful magic and got us fresh water.

Harrison took the hint and pulled me to him. "Thank you for saving me, Mandy."

"You're welcome."

His lips crashed into mine and we kissed, exploring each other, letting our tongues dance. I gently ran my tongue along his fangs, and he tightened his grip on my back.

Warrick joined us then. Sandwiching me between the two of them. His cock pressed into my back, and I rubbed shamelessly against Harrison's. My incubus reached around and slid his fingers against me, rubbing at my clit and sinking into me until I was trembling with the need for release.

"Why don't you take her now, Harrison," Warrick murmured, pulling his fingers out of me, gently coaching us as we came together for the first time.

The vampire helped me straddle him, and I sank down onto his cock, moaning happily. I was even happier when he thrust into me with Warrick's hands tight on my hips.

"Taste her," Warrick suggested.

"Mandy?" Harrison asked, voice breathy as he struggled to hang on.

"Yes, please." I'd asked for exactly this not long ago, and now I was getting what I wanted.

Harrison kissed my neck before gently biting me. This time he didn't hit me with all his power. I still saw stars as my entire body filled with liquid heat and electric pleasure.

Warrick hummed happily behind me, and Harrison groaned as he thrust into me once more before going rigid with his own release.

Before I could come down too far, Warrick trailed his fingers up my stomach, lighting me up again with his own powers. "Ready for round two?"

"Am I ever!" I was so not going to get any sleep tonight, but it would be so worth it.

"How many rounds do we get to go?" Harrison asked.

"As many as I can handle." I gave him a quick kiss on the lips before I gently lifted myself from his cock and threw myself at Warrick.

Eventually, we ended up in my bed. Harrison did me a solid before we finally passed out and gave me a little blood so I wouldn't hurt in the morning, and then we all curled into a pile. It might have been hellish getting here, but having these two men in my life was better than I could have possibly imagined.

CHAPTER 32

Price

Things were slowly getting back to a semblance of normal. Again. At least this time the pizza shop hadn't gotten trashed. In fact, while we'd been gone, a team of demons had taken it upon themselves to protect the shop from possible retaliation from the creature or anyone who might have sensed weakness.

The results had been mixed and, in hindsight, hilarious, except that Aaron's parents had tried to visit during the demonic protection racket and, well, I think they hated me even more now.

My regulars were getting a kick out of everything though. They thought I'd hired actors to really play up the new décor. I blessed Billy for his ability to think on his feet and keep the supernatural craziness under control.

Now it was just me and my guys protecting the shop from, fortunately, nothing too bad. Though the hunters had stopped by.

Apparently, they were back from Italy.

I eyed them nervously, but finally went over to say hello after Stacy had seated them. I'd given Mandy a two-week paid vacation because one, she deserved it, and two, she probably needed to spend every waking minute fucking her men or she wasn't going to be able to think straight when she came back to work. Not that I didn't approve. I was happy for her. I just knew how it was when you finally had everything you didn't even know you needed, and I wanted her to have time to enjoy herself so that she could focus on work when she came back. Also… she really deserved it. Like, she'd gone above and beyond what anyone could have expected. I just hoped once she got a handle on her new language powers, she decided to stick around for a while longer before she went off to conquer the world on her own.

"So, what's up, mates?" I asked the hunters once they'd given their orders.

"We wanted to thank you for helping Becca save us," Asher answered. "Also, we were spot checking places where the weird trucker activity had been the worst, and it seems like everything has gone back to normal. Gabriel must have done something to smooth things over."

"I believe Lucifer had a hand in that as well. Some sort of balance thing to keep it from seeming like one side or the other was doing too much on Earth." I shrugged. "Not that Lucifer cares, but I think Gabriel does. At least a little."

The hunters shifted uncomfortably at the mention of my demon, but they didn't comment.

"You're welcome on the assist," I added. "Glad we could get you all out. I hear you helped a lot during the fight, too. Brennan, especially, was grateful for your assistance."

That made them smile.

"Join us for a few minutes," Gael offered, sliding out a chair with his foot. "We should talk."

I sat and we chatted until someone yelped in the kitchen. Sighing, I stood. "I should probably make sure whatever showed up is friendly." Not that the wards would have let them in if they weren't, but sometimes demons got confused.

The hunters shook their heads in disbelief, but their pizza arrived as I left, and I figured they could get over it. So far, everyone else had.

***

Speaking of getting back to normal, or in this case not getting back to normal, the house had become a playground for hellhound puppies. They dashed in and out of the portal between my house and Ezra's domain as if it were just another door. This litter and another older one, raced around the house, phasing through doors like they did in Hell, blasting around outside playing with tennis balls, then careening back through the house, into the basement, and through the portal to wreak havoc in Ezra's stronghold.

"I can make them stop," Ezra said, looking a little harried as he attempted to corral them and failed.

"I don't think you can, mate. Instead, why don't you give me a kiss, since I know you're leaving for the night."

My demon prince smiled, and I lost myself in the depths of his eyes before he pressed his lips to mine. We kissed for a timeless moment before something crashed downstairs.

"I'll fix whatever it was," Ezra muttered, gave me one last kiss then hurried after the hellhounds.

Mal came out of the kitchen and arched an eyebrow. I shrugged.

"I need to head out for a little while." Mal wrapped me in his arms. "I'll see you soon."

"Thanks for a wonderful dinner." We kissed, then he left.

"I'll be right there," Aaron called.

I wondered what they were up to as Aaron gathered me close and kissed me soundly, before telling me he'd see me

261

later and following the vampire. Now I was extremely curious.

I noticed Brennan join Sabian in the kitchen. It really was too bad that the vampire couldn't eat his own cooking. Though he'd admitted once recently that he could experience the food more completely through our bonds than he used to be able to.

Sabian almost always did the dishes, despite having magical alternatives. He said he enjoyed helping around the house and doing the dishes the old-fashioned way saved our magical energy for when we might need it. Though, among those of us who could use magic, we were overpowered. Dishes wouldn't tax any of us. I wasn't going to argue with him, though. If he got enjoyment from it, I certainly didn't mind watching the sexy incubus in the kitchen. Hell, he usually cleaned shirtless. I could watch that all day every day and not get tired of it.

Truthfully, I was the one who felt like I wasn't pulling my weight. The guys took care of so much that I used to do. I wasn't complaining, mind, and it was nice not to have to take care of everything after a long day at the pizza shop. But still, sometimes I felt like I needed to do more.

Brennan joining Sabian was a little unusual. He preferred to do any cleaning magically, and when I saw him pick up a dish cloth to dry one of the pans that didn't go in the dishwasher, I almost gave in and eavesdropped through our connections.

I resisted. If he wanted to talk to me about whatever he was bringing to Sabian's attention, he would. And if not, it wasn't my business.

The light was long gone, but we had a mild winter evening, and I patted my leg, taking Mayhem outside for some air. Inferno shifted from his motorcycle form where he'd been asleep in the driveway and came over to my side, snuffling my arm. I leaned on the giant nightstallion while I watched Mayhem sniff around the front yard.

I lived outside of Santa Fe on the edge of the desert and my back was to the city. The first stars were lighting up the night sky, and I crossed my arms and stared out into the nothingness, contemplating the changes life had thrown at me in the last year. It was almost more than I could even comprehend, so I turned my attention to my present. Dwelling too much on the future or past had never been my favorite anyway.

A light breeze tickled along my neck and fluttered through Inferno's fiery mane. Mayhem lifted his little fluffy head and sniffed. I still couldn't figure out why the hellhound had taken a Pomeranian shape as his earthly form, but it suited him somehow.

As I was contemplating going back into the house, Sabian came over to join me.

"Are you up for some fun tonight?" He grinned at me, though his tone was oddly serious considering he was asking me about his favorite thing ever—sex.

"With you? Always." I grinned and straightened, stepping into the incubus's warmth.

He wrapped his arms around me and held me close.

"Actually, Brennan wants to try. He wants me there to help. Okay with you?"

I froze in surprise for a brief moment before warmth flooded through me. Brennan wanted to have sex with me? I never thought he'd ever want to go that far.

"I'd be honored," I admitted.

Sabian's expression brightened. "Good. We'll be inside whenever you're ready." He released me and went back into the house while I stared after him, still stunned. It made a lot of sense why Brennan would ask Sabian to be there. The incubus could sense what we were feeling, and always knew if someone would like something, even if the person themselves didn't know. He would be good support for the mage as he continued to recover from his trauma.

I turned back to Inferno and gave him a good scratch between his eyes. He lowered his head until he could share the air I breathed, inhaling as I exhaled. We stayed that way for another minute while Mayhem finished his patrol, and then I patted the nightstallion on the shoulder before Mayhem and I went inside.

The hellhound, expressing his trust in Sabian and Brennan, trotted into the living room while I headed to the bedroom.

Sabian had lit a few vanilla-scented candles on the table by the French doors, and only one low light was on to provide some illumination. Brennan sat in one of the armchairs.

I kicked off my shoes by the door then went over to the mage and held out my hand for his. His lack of hesitation when he slid his warm hand into mine filled me with a quiet peace.

"Hey, anything you want, you know that, right?"

"Thank you, Chris." He pulled me closer, so I stood between his knees. "Kiss me?"

"My pleasure."

Unless Mal had me tied, I wasn't normally very passive in bed. Even then, I was still in control despite the ropes that bound me into apparent submission. But Brennan had always needed me to be passive, and I'd always obliged.

Now I thought he was asking me for more. I glanced at Sabian, and he nodded, confirming my instincts. I leaned forward, threading the fingers of one hand into his hair and putting the other onto his waist.

Leaning forward, I hesitated, looking into his eyes.

He met my gaze, a smile tugging at the corners of his mouth.

Reassured by his expression, I pressed my lips to his. He responded, molding his lips to mine and tugging me closer. He scooted to the edge of the chair so we could be closer. Brennan was tall, and this position put us a little more even, though I had to bend over a little.

He dug his fingers into my back, clutching at me as we kissed. His trust warmed me and the love I could feel through our bond ignited a deep passion within me, heat pooling in my center and radiating through my body. I could have reached for Brennan through our bond, but I thought that might be too much, so I contained that urge.

Brennan parted his lips and pressed with his tongue. I opened for him, letting him explore, letting him lead for however long he wanted the kiss to continue.

After a time, Sabian touched both of our shoulders. I stepped away from the mage, panting. Brennan's eyes were wide, pupils dilated with lust and the low light. A slight frown marred his brow and I wanted to smooth it away but kept my hands to myself. Sabian had probably sensed the mage getting worried.

After a couple of deeper breaths, Brennan nodded. "That was really nice, thank you." His voice was rough with emotion.

Nice was inadequate to describe the kiss we'd just shared, but I understood what he meant, and what he was trying to say.

"Yeah, mate," I managed to get out, voice every bit as husky with lust as his was.

"Can I undress you?"

"Of course, Brennan." I stepped back so he could stand.

The mage gently guided me to the center of the room, running his hands over my shoulders and down my arms, trailing tendrils of fire along my skin. Once he reached my fingertips, he moved his hands to my hips and gently tugged my t-shirt out of my jeans. He caressed my skin as he lifted my shirt, exposing my stomach and the protective tattoos he and Lucifer had Mal had put on me. He leaned forward, pressing his lips to the pizza pentagram inscribed on my solar plexus.

His lips on my mark sent pleasant tingles through me and spread that sensation to my other men. They were all used to getting the occasional feedback from when I had sex and wouldn't remark on it.

Brennan took his time with my shirt, turning it into a sensual torture of sorts. He knew I wasn't the most patient, but he also knew I wouldn't rush him, and he used that to his advantage.

I groaned as he finally fully removed my t-shirt and unhooked my bra, baring my breasts much more quickly.

Taking a chance, I again threaded my fingers into his hair while he kissed my now exposed skin, tongue flicking at my nipples. I tightened my fingers, moaning encouragement.

"Sorry," I murmured, releasing him.

"It's okay," Brennan said, releasing my breast long enough to speak.

"I'll tell you if either are pushing too hard," Sabian said, reminding me that he was there.

"Thank you," Brennan said.

I echoed his words and went back to clutching my lover's hair as he paid exacting attention to my breasts.

"Fuck, that's good."

He trailed his fingers down my ribs, hands going to my belt. Slowly, torturously, he unthreaded the buckle then popped open the button on my jeans. I was practically squirming with need by the time the zipper followed. Brennan didn't take as long removing my pants, fortunately, and my undies went quickly until I stood in front of him, bare. He'd seen me naked many times, but something felt different in his gaze tonight.

"You are lovely, my exorcist," he murmured.

That didn't seem to need a response, so I simply waited.

"Brennan, go ahead and get undressed," Sabian suggested when the mage seemed indecisive.

I nodded, and he quickly shed his clothing, before holding out a hand and leading me to the bed. I went ahead and pulled back the sheets and sank down onto the comfortable mattress, happy to see the evidence of Brennan's desire in his arousal as he stood there.

Brennan glanced at Sabian.

"I've got a suggestion," the incubus said softly. "We usually make Chris come all sorts of times before we take our turn, but, I think, you should go first, Brennan. Get your pleasure first. It will be vastly different from your normal experiences and maybe help."

The mage looked at me. "Is that okay?"

"Of course, Brennan. I'm so happy you want to do this with me. That's a pleasure in and of itself, and I'm happy to go second."

"Okay." He crawled up on the bed with me, gently pushing on my shoulder so I laid back.

I spread my knees and waited for him to make the next move. I was already dripping wet. It wouldn't take much for me to be ready to comfortably take the mage, even without having my own orgasms first.

He ran his fingers down my stomach, over my short patch of not bleached-blond hair and trailed his fingers over my wet pussy, gently caressing.

"That feels good," I encouraged him.

He slid a finger through my folds, getting it wet before sliding it inside me and curling a bit. I couldn't help the groan that escaped my lips and the soft buck of my hips, wanting more.

Brennan stuck to the plan Sabian had outlined, getting me worked up, and ready for him, but pulling away before I was ready to come.

"Good?" he asked uncertainly.

"If you are, I'm ready, Brennan." I tried to soften the lust in my voice to a lower intensity, but the desire was still there.

He took a breath and positioned himself above me.

I smiled at him, though I really wanted to grab his hips and slam him into me. That wasn't what he needed. Maybe someday.

"Go ahead, Brennan. You're ready," Sabian encouraged.

He pressed into me, stretching me and filling me, and I didn't even have to pretend at how good it felt to have him inside me.

"Mind if I grab your hips?"

"Go ahead, Chris," Brennan breathed. He took a few deep breaths and focused on my face when he began to move after I put my hands on him.

The trust he showed me made me feel like the most special person on all the planes at that moment. I couldn't even describe what Brennan coming to me like this meant.

Sabian moved over next to the bed and ran his fingers down Brennan's back when the mage froze after a few thrusts. Something eased in the mage. I wasn't sure what Sabian had done, but the look on Brennan's face was all gratitude.

"It's okay," Sabian murmured. "It's Chris."

Brennan exhaled and leaned down, pressing his lips to mine, before he thrust into me in earnest.

It wasn't long before I was crying out in pleasure, not far off from my own climax. I was determined to let

Brennan go first, though. Sabian sensed this and touched my shoulder, easing my energy a bit.

Brennan was gasping now, and I cried out his name as he shuddered, thrusting one last time and squeezing his eyes shut.

A few tears leaked from his eyes, but when he opened them, he smiled at me. One of the few genuine smiles I'd ever seen from my mage.

"Your turn," he whispered.

"Mmm, looking forward to it."

Brennan slipped out of me and replaced his cock with his fingers, curling them expertly until I was crying out again, writhing on the bed, so close to coming it was almost painful.

The mage, damn him, slowed. I snapped open my eyes and glared.

He laughed. I wanted to be annoyed, but the sound was music to my ears, so while I kept glaring, there was no real heat behind the expression, and he knew it.

Finally, Brennan picked up the speed again, and this time he didn't stop until I shouted with my release.

He gave me a few extra strokes, before slipping his fingers out of me and curling his body around me while I trembled in reaction.

"Let's do that again, soon," Brennan whispered.

"Any time, Brennan, my love," I replied. "Any time."

Every moment with my men was special and even sacred to me. I loved them all wholly, yet each relationship was a little different. That they all got along with and respected each other made this life we were carving out together even more spccial, and I couldn't wait to see what the future had in store for all of us.

The End

Author's Note

Thank you so much for reading my reverse harem tale! More is coming soon! Reviews are so very important and are greatly appreciated! Even a line or two will do!

About the Author

Dakota has two passions in life: writing and cinnamon tea. Tea so strong she ought to be able to see her future when she drinks it, and the writing? Well, she hopes it makes you see stars when you read it. She creates reverse harem romance novels filled with things that go bump in the night. That handsome werewolf walking down the street? The suave vampire you're just dying to get a taste of? You'll find them enraptured by charming, smart ladies ready to make those bad boys work for their affection. When not writing, Dakota can be found on the back of a horse out on the trail or tending the animals on her farm.

Other Works

Mountain Magic Trilogy (complete)

Becoming
Demon's Touch
Reckoning

Ocean Enchantment Trilogy

Siren's Catch
Siren's Song
Siren's Storm

Pizza Shop Exorcist (complete)

The Price of Possession
The Price of Exorcism
The Price of Magic
The Price of Souls
The Price of Rebellion

Horsemen Against the Apocalypse Duet

Seeking War
Apocalypse Interrupted

Dreambound Trilogy (Complete)

Nightmare's Dance
Nightmare's Fall
Nightmare's Flight

Pizza Shop Monster Hunter
Monster's Price (stands alone)